Contents

ONE

Tatum

THE SKYSCRAPERS OF MANHATTAN GLEAMED UNDER the bright sun as it peaked over the horizon. My office faced the west, so I got to see winter sunsets when the sun sank behind the horizon and disappeared.

My hand moved across the document I was marking up, filling my silent office with the quiet scratching of the pen tip against the thick paper. Sometimes I was in the mood for dead silence, focusing on my work with such discipline I could rip a hole in it with my pen alone. And other times, like today, I was in the mood for a quiet tune.

I grabbed the remote, hit a button, and Frank Sinatra's voice filled my space.

Floor-to-ceiling windows took up the back wall of my office, and my white desk matched the bookshelves on either side. The dark wood at my feet was covered by a gray rug, and two blue armchairs faced my desk with a white coffee table in the center.

It wasn't dark and foreboding like most offices I'd been to. My goal wasn't to intimidate potential clients and partners, but to expose them to the sleekness and elegance I preferred. There was always a fresh vase of flowers on the coffee table.

It was one luxury I couldn't live without.

The door to my office opened, but I didn't look up from my work, knowing exactly who it was.

Jessica walked inside and set the coffee cup and saucer on the edge of my desk. A silver spoon rested on the white plate. It clanked from her jittery movements. She was either experiencing a caffeine crash, or she was just nervous.

Since it was her first week, I knew which one it was.

"Here you are, Ms. Titan." She moved the cup closer toward me, spilling a drop on the white wood. "Oh god, I'm so sorry." She patted it dry with a napkin.

"That's alright." I smiled with my eyes peering down. I remembered my first day of work. I had been just as nervous as she was. Before I lost my train of thought, I finished what I was doing and dropped the silver pen that was the perfect width for my slim fingers.

That's when I noticed the cream-colored coffee.

Jessica had just turned away to head back to her desk.

"Jessica." I called her back without raising my voice.

"Yes, Ms. Titan?"

"Call me Titan." It saved time instead of stating two words every time she tried to address me. My first name was rarely uttered by anyone, only those who crossed the line of my inner circle. And even then, they usually called me by a nickname instead.

"Oh…sorry." She cringed, her hands balling into fists at her own stupidity.

"It's okay, Jessica. These things take time." I looked her in the eye and smiled. "I like my coffee black with two sugars." I pushed the cup closer to her, sliding it across the textured wood until it was easily accessible.

She realized her third mistake with another cringe. "Of course. I must have gotten confused with…" She trailed off, unable to find an excuse for her lack of commitment. "I'll fix this right now."

"Thank you."

She picked up the saucer and the cup, breathing

harder than necessary. It seemed like she was a soldier in the military and I was her drill sergeant. She was scared to make the slightest mistake because that would cost her ten push-ups.

"Can I give you some advice, Jessica?"

"Of course." She gripped the saucer closer to her, standing at attention with her eyes trained on me. They were bigger than usual, a permanent look of surprise on her face.

"It's okay to make mistakes." Throughout my life, I learned more from my failures than my successes. When I accomplished a goal, there was nothing to gain from it. But my failures always led to greater success down the road. Failures were the moments that stuck with you, the ones that kept you up late at night. "But it's not okay to repeat them."

She nodded slightly, expressing her understanding.

"I give new employees two weeks to learn the ropes. So take a deep breath and relax. The more you overthink it, the more mistakes you'll make. Just be confident."

"Of course," she said breathlessly. "I guess…never mind."

"What?" Vague comments and vague questions irritated me. I liked conversation to be clear and concise. When there were misinterpretations, that led to wasted time. And there was nothing I hated more than wasting time.

"I'm just intimidated by you, Titan." She finally broke our locked gazes. "Extremely."

"You know what I do when I'm intimidated by someone?"

She let out an involuntary chuckle.

I raised an eyebrow.

"Oh…you aren't joking."

I lowered my eyebrow and suppressed the little smile that wanted to form on my lips. "I give them a reason to be intimidated by me. So, Jessica, do your worst."

———

I FINISHED THREE MEETINGS, had lunch, and now I sorted through my emails and filtered out the rest of my week. Work never rested, and unfortunately, I didn't either. There was a club get-together this Saturday, and I'd have to make sure I swung by. After a few drinks, I'd end up on the dance floor. And when I spent the night on the dance floor, I always had a good time.

Jessica rapped her knuckles against the glass door

before she stepped into my office. "Titan, I have Diesel Hunt's assistant on the phone."

I knew Diesel Hunt, not by face, but reputation. He was one of the many billionaires in this city, though definitely one of the youngest. At the age of thirty-five, he possessed more wealth than most people could even grasp. He was ruthless, cold, and determined.

I respected him.

Jessica continued when she knew I was listening. "He wants to schedule a meeting."

I'd never met Diesel Hunt, and our businesses had nothing in common. Whatever he wanted was a mystery to me. "What is it regarding?"

"She didn't say."

"Then you need to ask, Jessica. When you present information to me, I want all the facts right then and there."

"Of course, Titan. You got it." She pulled the glass door shut and walked away.

I had four assistants, all of them handling different zones. One focused on my schedule, one focused on my transportation, another handled my personal agenda, and the remaining floated in between.

Jessica came back five minutes later. "She said

Diesel Hunt wants to discuss a business opportunity with you."

Without knowing the sound of his voice, I could feel his arrogance. Did I look like someone who needed a business opportunity? There weren't enough hours in the day for me to manage my own empire. To expand with someone else didn't suit my financial interests. Like a lone wolf, I did everything by myself. "Tell him no."

"No?" she asked.

"Yes. Tell him I'm not interested."

"Uh…" She held the door open in her palm, her silver bracelet clanking slightly against the silver cylinder that stretched from top to bottom and acted as the door handle. My office was modern and open, with glass walls that divided employees from one another, giving them silence for phone calls but not much privacy. "You want me to say that to Diesel Hunt?"

I swallowed my annoyance at her uncertainty. Diesel Hunt had a powerful reputation that stretched to every single person in the city, and perhaps, the country. He was a man with a strong fascination for cars and women, like all other rich men. No wasn't a word he heard very often.

Too bad.

"Yes, tell him I'm not interested."

After two heartbeats passed, she walked out.

———

I LET myself inside and stepped into the spacious penthouse that overlooked the river. The tinted windows didn't hide the breathtaking view of the sun disappearing from the world's eyesight. "It's me."

Thorn sat on the couch in the living room, his back facing me. He held up his glass to greet me. "I've got your drink right here—with an orange peel and a cherry." He shook the glass, the ice swirling inside with the dark whiskey.

"And you have my attention." I took the seat beside him and crossed my legs. I snatched the glass out of his hand and took a deep drink, downing it like water instead of whiskey.

In a navy blue suit with a matching tie, Thorn sat with his leg crossed. His ankle rested on the opposite knee, and his crisp suit lacked a single wrinkle. Pressed by professionals, his clothes exuded distinct power. He brought his glass to his lips and downed it. When he was finished, he licked his lips. "I don't understand your fascination with Old Fashioneds. Too strong and too sweet at the same time."

"Really?" I took another sip. "Not strong enough if you ask me."

"I would have made you a double, but I wasn't sure if you drove the Bugatti."

"Nope. My driver dropped me off."

"In that case, I'll make the next one a triple." He rested his arm across the back of the couch, taking up twice the amount of space he needed.

I slipped off my heels and ran my fingers through my hair, no longer required to put up the front I constantly presented to the rest of the world. Thorn had seen me at my best and my worst. Secrets didn't leave our hideaway. "Got something for me?"

"You know me." With a chiseled jawline and pretty eyes, he looked at me with a slight smile, like he had something fun to share. "Bruce Carol's new company is rumored to be a big mistake."

"Really?" I kept my fingers around my glass, my nails tapping against the condensation. "I've heard otherwise."

"He's putting all the PR out there to disguise it as a success. But I've seen the books."

"How?"

He shrugged. "I don't kiss and tell. You know that."

I did—all too well. "Is it terminal?"

"Definitely. I give it six months."

"Really?" I pulled my knees toward my body and pivoted myself to look at him.

"Really." Now he wore his boyish smile, looking like a childhood friend rather than a grown business associate. "He invested more than he should, and his other businesses aren't doing so hot. It's only a matter of time."

"You know I'm not interested in buying other businesses and reinventing them."

"But this is a money grab," he said. "Meet with him in private and find the right price. You could take this before it hits the market."

My eyes narrowed as my interest was piqued. Money wasn't the most important thing to me. Getting a great deal was. Like a sickness, it consumed me. If this really was a great business opportunity, I wanted it.

I wanted them all.

"It's ironic." I took another drink until the glass was empty. I returned it to the coffee table, feeling the warmth burn my throat and stomach on its way down. The second a strong drink was sitting inside me, I could think even more clearly than usual. "Diesel Hunt contacted my office today. Wanted to discuss a business opportunity."

"Really?" Thorn cocked his head, his eyes narrowing. "He doesn't do business with anyone."

"I'm aware."

"And that can only mean he wants to buy something from you."

"That's what I concluded as well." Thorn and I were of one mind. It explained our deep connection, our bond that extended beyond our business relationship.

"When are you meeting him?"

"I'm not."

He held his glass close to his chest, his eyes focused on me with devout attention. "You aren't? What does that mean?"

"I said no."

All seriousness died away, and he was left with a grin that would soon turn into a laugh. "You said no?"

I gave a slight nod.

"To Diesel Hunt."

I nodded again.

He finally let the laugh escape his chest. "Man, bet he didn't like that one bit. The word no isn't in his vocabulary."

"Now it is. Looks like he learned something."

Thorn laughed again before he took a drink. "I

doubt that will be the end of him. When he wants something, he gets it."

"Well, when I want something, I get it too."

"Maybe he's met his match. Are you still the keynote speaker this Friday?"

"Yep." I ran my fingers through my hair again, feeling the softness stretch down to my shoulders.

"He might be there."

"Men like Hunt don't attend business conferences. I'm only speaking as a favor."

"He might if he knows you're there."

"Well, I'll keep him on my radar. Though I'm not even sure what he looks like."

"How do you not know what he looks like?" Thorn asked incredulously.

"Because I've been too busy running an empire to care about the appearance of my competitors."

He rested his arm over the back of the couch, holding his now empty glass. "Well, as busy as he is, I'm sure he's taken the extra five seconds to care about yours."

TWO

Hunt

———

N<small>ATALIE</small> <small>WALKED</small> <small>INTO</small> <small>MY</small> <small>OFFICE</small> <small>IN</small> <small>SKY-HIGH</small> heels. I didn't have a dress code for my building, but I asked my assistants to always wear black. The color suited the gray walls, as well as my office. "Sir, Titan's assistant said she wasn't interested."

Not interested?

What kind of answer was that?

I felt the muscles of my jaw clench. My palm automatically rubbed across my chin to suppress its appearance. My five o'clock shadow was already coming in, darkening my face even though I'd shaved that morning. My annoyance didn't come from an inflated ego, just surprise.

No one ever said no to me.

"Put me through directly."

Natalie nodded in understanding before she left my office.

I stared at my phone as I waited for it to ring. I was in the middle of writing an email, but now it was forgotten. My cell phone lit up with a text message from Pine, but that was immediately filtered into a different compartment in my brain, where all things unimportant were stored.

The phone rang.

I picked it up and heard Natalie over the line. "I have Diesel Hunt for Ms. Titan." Her feminine voice contained a slight hint of urgency.

Titan's assistant faltered, and her lack of confidence suggested she was new. "I'm sorry, does he have an appointment?"

"I don't need an appointment." My mobile phone screen filled up with ten different emails as my life carried on. I'd stopped my world to make this phone call, and I didn't appreciate being told to wait.

Titan's assistant paused again. "Uh…one moment, please."

Natalie got off the line.

I sat there for a full minute.

A long-ass minute.

No one had ever made me wait this long for anything.

Ms. Titan was playing with fire right now.

Titan's assistant came back to the phone, and I was disappointed when I heard her voice. "What is this regarding?"

Is this a joke? "I'd like to speak to her about the business opportunity mentioned yesterday."

"She needs you to be more specific."

I ground my teeth together. "Once she's on the line, I'll be as specific as she likes."

"I'm sorry, Mr. Hunt. Ms. Titan isn't interested in unsolicited proposals at this time. She appreciates the call and wishes you the best."

Unsolicited proposals?

What the fuck?

"Put her through——"

"Have a good day, sir." She hung up.

She hung up on me.

Me.

———

WHEN THE WAITRESS set our drinks down, her skirt lifted right up, exposing her panties so I could see them.

It was definitely on purpose.

But I didn't look. It didn't impress me when a

woman put everything on display to get my attention. Subtly was sexy. Overwhelming nakedness was not. I wanted a woman to want me, not throw herself at me without an ounce of class.

Pine's eyes followed the woman as she walked away, leaving us in our booth in the club. The lights were low, and the music was high. Women and couples danced on the floor, and people downed their drinks like water. Two women sat on either side of Pine, and his arms were draped over their shoulders. Mike was in the same situation. "What's your problem?"

My eyes turned to Pine. "I don't have a problem."

"A beautiful woman just showed you her ass, and you didn't even look."

"I've seen lots of beautiful asses."

"And you look awfully lonely over there by yourself." He pulled his arm away from the blonde and positioned her toward me. "There you go. That's better."

My arm was resting over the back of the couch, but I didn't lean into her. I didn't need Pine to get me a girl, and I certainly didn't want a girl he'd already claimed. Leftovers weren't my thing. "I tried talking to Tatum Titan today. Couldn't get her on the phone for two seconds."

"Tatum Titan?" he asked, knowing exactly who that was. "Really?"

I nodded. "My assistant tried to schedule a meeting with her twice. She said she wasn't interested."

"Is she stupid?"

"I called her myself... Still didn't get her attention."

Pine whistled under his breath. "Damn...that must have ticked you off."

I gave him a glare.

"And I was right."

"I don't understand this woman. She's got a failing business, and I want to buy it from her. If she weren't so stubborn, she could at least hear my offer."

"Sounds like she doesn't want an offer."

She should want any offer she could get from me. I drank my glass and scanned the club, seeing the beautiful women in their tight dresses and heels. I could go home with someone tonight, or I could not. Didn't make much of a difference to me. When you had too much of one thing, it turned bland and stale. It'd been a long time since my senses had come to life. It was the same routine every single day. I was living in the fast lane, but I was going at such a breakneck speed it actually felt slow.

"What are you going to do now?"

"Why would I do anything?" I felt the blonde scoot closer to me and rest her hand on my chest. I didn't push her off, but I didn't pull her closer either.

"Because I know you, Hunt. You don't stop until you get what you want. And the fact that this woman refuses to give it to you...just makes you want it more."

All I felt for that woman was pure annoyance. I didn't even care about her company that much. I just saw a quick buck and decided to make it. I assumed anyone would be happy to rid themselves of a failing business. Her cold and indifferent response surprised me because I'd never experienced it before. But now I wanted her company even more...just to prove to her she shouldn't have rejected me so easily.

"She's speaking at the Business Coalition Conference on Friday."

"She is?" I already was planning on attending.

"Yep. And I hope she wears a skirt because she's fiiiiine. Got the nicest legs I've ever seen."

Couldn't care less about her legs.

"And her ass...damn." Pine continued on even though he already had a girl to take home.

Beautiful or not, it was irrelevant. All I wanted

from her was an acquisition. "When did you see her?"

"She had a meeting with my father about a year ago. I was in the office when she walked by. My dad said she's the smartest person he's ever met…and that's saying something because he says everyone's an idiot—me included."

I stared across the club but didn't focus on anything in particular.

"She's the richest woman in the world—pretty impressive."

Richest woman in the world?

"She's number eleven on the Forbes list. Just a few spots lower than you."

I hadn't known anything about her personally up until that point, just heard her name here and there. My interest grew when I thought I could capitalize on her existing product. Deep inside, I was impressed, but I did my best not to show it.

"So I guess I'm not surprised by the way she brushed you off. She probably has an ego."

I'd be surprised if she didn't.

"How about you—"

"Did you see the Yankees game last night?" I was done talking about Titan. She'd occupied my thoughts enough for the day.

————

MY DRIVER PULLED up to the hotel and opened the door for me.

The second I stepped out, people snapped pictures of me on their phones. A reporter leaned in with a tape recorder right in my face. "What's next for Hunt Auto?"

I'd been doing this my whole life, so I took the attention in stride. I didn't outright smile, but I wore a welcoming expression. I held up my hand in the form of a wave and kept walking, brushing them off without looking like an asshole while doing it.

I walked inside and buttoned the front of my suit. Eyes were on me immediately, recognizing me in an instant. Most of the people there were aspiring entrepreneurs, along with a couple veterans. I shook hands with a few men then moved on.

The keynote speech was taking place in the ballroom, and I slipped in just as they made her introduction.

"As the principal owner of one of the largest beauty and cosmetic companies in the world, Tatum Titan is the richest woman in the world with a net worth of forty-four billion dollars. She started her first company at the age of fifteen and has increased her presence in the capital sphere ever since. A powerful force in business, she's invested her interests into foreign markets, as well as clean energy here in the United States. Her company, Illuminance, is the first energy company to create solar energy panels exterior to buildings, allowing homes to skip the solar-panel roofs for an exterior pod. Her company's research has also made solar energy more affordable than traditional sources. Help me welcome Ms. Titan to the stage." The man clapped before he walked away from the podium, giving her the entire stage.

The audience clapped along enthusiastically.

My eyes searched the bottom of the stairs until I found her. In five-inch stilettos, she ascended the stairs without grabbing on to the rail for balance. Her calf muscles tightened with her movements, her toned and slender legs long and luscious. The pencil skirt she wore fit her waistline perfectly, accentuating the feminine curves of her body.

When she reached the top, she walked to the podium and rested her hands on the surface. Her posture was perfect, her shoulders back and her head held high. She didn't look down once, her eyes on the crowd in front of her—fearless.

She wore a deep navy top that was tucked in to her skirt. All the buttons were fastened, and the shirt stretched across the swell of her breasts. Her skin was tanned, kissed by the sun. For someone who spent most of her time working, she obviously spent time outdoors. A curtain of dark strands, her long hair was curled and shiny. Light makeup was on her face, just enough to accentuate her features but not overwhelm them.

I was forced to agree with what Pine had said.

She was everything he described her to be.

My eyes trailed over her body, and I tuned out all the words she said. She discussed her business ventures, the struggles of opening her first store, and her journey to becoming a powerful capitalist and brand.

But my eyes cared more about the hollow of her throat, the smooth skin that would be perfect for a man's tongue. Her left hand was absent of a wedding ring. In fact, she didn't wear any jewelry at all.

If I saw her on the street, I wouldn't have known she was such a successful entrepreneur.

She worked the stage like she owned it, making the audience laugh at times and take her seriously at others. She knew exactly how to engage with her audience, to make them feel exactly what she wanted them to feel.

She looked carefree.

I sat in the back row and watched from a safe distance, but my eyes were entranced by the way her hips swayed from side to side. She didn't drag her feet when she walked. She worked her heels like they were flat sandals.

And she had the kind of confidence that rivaled my own.

I'd never seen a woman quite like this. I met other women in business who were successful, and I'd met women who were just as beautiful.

But never at the same time.

She was a different breed.

When she finished her presentation, she opened the floor to questions. People fired off right away, some with good questions and others with mediocre ones. It was obvious who were experienced business owners and who didn't know how to add two numbers together.

One reporter in the front raised his hand.

Tatum focused her gaze on him. "Go ahead."

He stood up so everyone else in the auditorium could hear him. "As a woman entering her thirties, does this mean you'll be putting your business on hold to start a family? Or is having a family a goal you don't value?"

My eyes narrowed at the backhanded insult posed in the question. It was sexist, to say the least. I wasn't even a woman, and the question annoyed me. My gaze turned back to Tatum, wondering how she would handle it.

Her face softened into a smile, and it looked so convincing I would have thought it was real. "It's very rare that I encounter a reporter who's so concerned with my reproductive health. My ovaries are in great shape, thank you for asking. I'm not entering menopause for at least twenty years, so I've got some time." She scanned the audience again, not breaking her stride or confidence. "Any other questions?"

Both corners of my mouth rose into a smile, admiring the way she brushed off the question without really addressing it. She made the guy look like an ass even after he'd already made himself look like an ass.

Another reporter stood up—another male one. "How does it feel to be the richest woman in the world?"

I actually rolled my eyes at that one.

She wore that same diplomatic smile. "I'd

imagine it feels the same as being the richest man in the world."

I smiled again, noting her subtle fire and hostility. She insulted people without making it obvious, fighting her battles with an indirect touch that was more powerful than a punch in the face.

And I respected her for it.

THREE

Tatum

———————

LUCAS HUNG NEARBY, ACTING AS MY PRIVATE driver and bodyguard. He was there only for show because I certainly didn't need a man to fight my battles. When I hired him, I just needed him to navigate me through the city so I could keep working in the back seat, but he offered more extensive services. After working for me for years, he'd developed a strong sense of protectiveness over me.

Loyalty was far more valuable than a paycheck, so I accepted his offer.

Jessica and Courtney trailed behind me, their notepads ready for anything that I could possibly need. They stood in silence, scanning the room and informing me of anyone important coming my way. They were my professional entourage, providing an intimidating circle that made business associates think twice before approaching me.

If I were alone, I wouldn't be able to bat the flies away.

A man in a black suit approached me from against the back of the auditorium. His suit stretched over his strong shoulders, his tailored outfit obviously the work of Armani. A powerful body was hinted underneath the collared shirt and jacket, and I suspected there was a wall of muscle tucked away. I only allowed him a short glance, keeping my thoughts and reactions buried within my green eyes. I didn't recognize his face, and I wondered if he was an aspiring businessman.

With looks and confidence like that, he'd probably make it.

Jessica interposed her body in his way, cutting him off before he could walk up to me. "Hello, sir. Can I help you?"

He stared at her with his hands resting in his pockets. The look wasn't hostile, but his deep brown eyes exerted so much power it filled the room like humidity. He never tore his look away from her, silently commanding her to step aside.

Jessica visibly shrank before my eyes, turning into melted butter right there on the floor. Whether it was his obvious attractiveness or his radiating power, it wasn't clear what made her take a large step to the left.

My assistant needed to get a backbone.

Now there was nothing in this man's way, so I faced him with my hands together at my waist. I didn't flinch the way Jessica did, but I'd be lying if I said I wasn't affected by his stern countenance. He had a square jaw that was chiseled into masculine perfection. A five o'clock shadow sprinkled his jaw even though it wasn't even noon yet. His cream-colored collared shirt was pressed over a hard chest, the muscles of his pecs highlighted beneath the fabric. His eyes were brown like a hot cup of coffee on a fall afternoon, but they shone with a depth as cold as a winter morning. He stared at me with the same hard expression he gave my assistant, not the least bit intimidated by me. Men surveyed me with mixed opinions, some respecting me and others doubting my work. Most men were sexist without even realizing it. So far, I couldn't tell how this man viewed me.

Words weren't spoken, but a conversation carried on between us. It was a silent battle of power. He seemed to be testing me, but I was also testing him.

The longer neither one of us spoke but kept our certainty, the more assured we seemed.

I had all day.

He pulled his right hand out of his pocket and extended it to me. "Diesel Hunt."

Now I understood the subtle hostility. I took his hand, feeling his powerful wrist under my grasp. I purposely squeezed my hand a little harder than his, needing to project the same kind of strength that oozed from his pores. "Tatum Titan."

His fingertips were callused as if they hit the keyboard for too many hours of the day. His skin was warm to the touch, his testosterone-pumped muscles producing heat like a furnace in the middle of January. His hand was significantly bigger than mine, overpowering my grasp with brute size. I made up for petiteness with strength, giving him a harder squeeze before I dropped my hand.

I'd heard the rumors about him. That he was tall and handsome and a bit of a ladies' man. Usually, rumors were exaggerated, and sometimes, completely false. But everything I had heard about him was dead-on.

He was something else.

He didn't return his hand to his pocket but rested it at his side. "I enjoyed your speech."

And the asshole continued to undermine me—unsuccessfully. "I doubt a man as experienced as yourself learned anything new."

His chocolate-colored eyes narrowed, focusing on my lips for just an instant. "That's a compliment coming from you, Ms. Titan."

I let my lips soften into a smile.

"But you must not think that highly of me if I can't get you on the phone for two minutes."

I wasn't stupid enough to think this topic wouldn't arise. He obviously had his determination set on me, interested in one of my businesses. I liked to work alone, and from what I understood, he did too. "I have two minutes now, Mr. Hunt."

His eyes concentrated on my own, and he took a slight step forward. He was definitely in my personal space, his power infecting every corner of the room. Like a gentle hum in my ear, I could actually hear it. With a height that far exceeded my own, even in heels, he had to be at least six foot three.

I liked tall men.

"I'm a man who lasts longer than two minutes, Ms. Titan."

Whether he meant to make the inference on purpose, I picked up on the innuendo. He exuded sex by the gallon, and I was surprised he didn't smell like a woman's perfume right then. He probably had women battling over who could give him head first. Women were a commodity he had in surplus, a product that never expired.

"Let's have lunch. You must be hungry after that lecture."

"I have plans for lunch."

"Then let's schedule something for tomorrow at my office."

I stopped myself from laughing, but I couldn't stop myself from smiling. "Mr. Hunt, I'm not interested in any kind of business venture with you. I'm flattered, nonetheless."

He didn't show a hint of anger, but he hardly blinked as he looked at me. "It's not smart to turn down an offer you haven't heard. Rule number one of business school."

"I wouldn't know—I didn't go to college." I wasn't like the rest of my peers with their Ivy League degrees. I started working in the industry before I became a legal adult. While there was always new material to learn in any environment, a formal education seemed boring to me. I preferred a hands-on approach to life. There were some things you couldn't learn from books—like how to survive.

He glanced at my lips again, this time staring at

them longer than before. He obviously didn't care if I noticed before he looked me in the eye again, as confident as ever. "I'm interested in your publishing house. It's a failing business, if you didn't know."

I didn't know how he got his information, but that didn't matter. He was right on the money. "I'm aware of my finances. Thank you for your concern." I didn't like to be questioned about my choices. I wouldn't be in the position I was in now if I didn't trust my instincts.

"Then you should listen to my offer."

"I'm not in the market to sell." If he pushed hard, I'd push harder back. I glanced at my watch before I looked at his concentrated expression once more. "Your two minutes are up, Mr. Hunt. Take care."

I pivoted away from him, maintaining the same posture I did anytime I was in the public eye. My shoulders were back, my chest was out, and I glided on my heels. I wore stilettos every hour of the day except when I was finally alone in my penthouse. They were like a second skin, and walking barefoot felt almost unsteady.

Diesel Hunt didn't stop my exit, but his eyes burned into my back. I could feel his presence surround me like a heavy blanket, nearly suffocating me. The heat from his gaze licked my body like flames from a hearth. I could even feel his look on my ass.

Diesel Hunt wasn't an enemy I wanted to have, but he wasn't an appropriate business partner either. Hopefully, that interaction was the last one we would ever have.

But I suspected it wasn't.

FOUR

Hunt

I SPUN THE PEN IN MY FINGERS AS I LOOKED ACROSS
the city. My legs were crossed, my suit fit me like a
glove, and I stared at the skyscrapers I owned.
Manhattan wasn't mine, but I was an ambitious man
with a driven mind. One day, I would own
everything.

And everyone.

I had a few meetings that morning, but my head
wasn't in the game. My thoughts kept drifting to a
queen in stilettos, a woman who countered my
confidence with her own majesty. She was so certain
in her worth that she assumed I couldn't afford her.

She was wrong.

Face-to-face, I noticed the corners of her mouth.
Her skin was creamy white, and I imagined how soft
it would feel if I brushed the back of my finger across

her cheek. My jaw ached when I thought about those lips, that plump and pink mouth that would feel good all over my body.

She had almond-shaped eyes that were distinctly feminine and accented the green color of her irises. As womanly as she was, she showcased the kind of presence a king held every time he addressed his subjects. I'd never met a woman more beautiful, more exquisite, and so abundantly powerful at the same time.

Jesus Christ.

She turned me down without caring about the money on the table. She was so wealthy, so suave, that she didn't care about missing a deal. She was headstrong and stubborn, playing by her own rules and not even entertaining mine. When I suggested she come to my office, she nearly laughed.

I spotted it.

Women threw themselves at me constantly, wanting to be a visitor in my bed for the night. They wanted to ride on my expensive yacht in the Caribbean. They wanted a glimpse of the fast lifestyle that I experienced on a daily basis.

They never said no to me.

I couldn't remember the last time I heard the word.

But Ms. Titan wasn't impressed by me. She didn't care about my money. She didn't care about my line of cars and yachts. There was nothing I had that she didn't already possess.

Except my bed.

I continued to spin the pen in my fingertips, thinking about those long legs underneath that skirt. She was five years younger than me, but just as successful. It was hard to earn my respect, but she'd earned it a million times over.

She was magnificent.

Natalie knocked on my door before she stepped inside my office. "Sir, your next meeting is in five minutes."

My back was to her, and I continued to stare at the city, knowing Titan's building was just a few blocks away. "Cancel it."

Natalie didn't question my decision, knowing that was a big mistake. "Shall I reschedule?"

"For tomorrow." I rose out of my chair and buttoned the front of my suit. "Cancel everything for the next hour. I have somewhere to be." I knew exactly where I was going, but now I wasn't entirely sure why I was going.

I told myself it was just a business opportunity, a

way to steal a dying business and turn it into a thriving one.

But I'd never lied to myself—and I didn't want to start now.

———

JESSICA'S JAW actually dropped when she saw me standing in front of her desk.

When it was obvious she wasn't going to say anything, I took the reins. "Diesel Hunt here for Tatum Titan."

Jessica continued to stare at me before she finally grasped this was reality—and she was still staring at me. "Uh, of course." She frantically flipped through her schedule book before she realized she was already on the correct date and flipped back. "Uh…"

My hands slid into my pockets. "I don't have an appointment." If Titan wasn't going to give me any of her time, fine. I'd just take it.

"Titan doesn't see anyone without an appointment…"

Until now. "I'll take a seat." I sat in the comfortable lobby outside her office. She had two large glass doors that led to her expansive space. I didn't look for her because I didn't want to be caught staring. Her couches were gray and the walls were white. Vases of flowers were everywhere, and nothing but the sound of keyboards and ringing phones filled the air. Three other assistants kept looking at me, recognizing me instantly.

Jessica walked into the office and returned a few minutes later. She approached me with her fingers interlocked tightly. She was a nervous mess, and it made me wonder why Titan employed someone so unsure of herself. It was a direct contradiction to her own personality and work ethic. "She's unavailable."

Man, this woman was infuriating. "I'll wait."

Jessica glanced at the door then looked at me again. "Uh…"

I watched her, hostility in my gaze. If Titan wanted to get rid of me, she'd have to see me. She'd wasted enough of my time dismissing me. Now it was my turn to waste her time.

Jessica walked back into the office. She was gone longer this time before she came out. "She'll see you in ten minutes." She walked back to her seat and sat down, her head bowed and her eyes concentrated on her desk.

A smile formed on my lips, the sensation of success running through my veins. No one said no to

Diesel Hunt—not even Tatum Titan. I always got my way eventually.

I suspected she made me wait ten minutes out of principle, just to retain some of the power in the situation. The second she agreed to meet with me, she lost some of her leverage over me.

I loved this game.

Jessica spoke to Titan on the phone before she approached me on the couch. "Titan will see you now." She opened the glass door for me.

I dropped my smile and walked inside, surrounded by the pleasing aesthetics of her office. Her entire back wall was a large window that overlooked the city, giving her the exact same view I got from my office. A white desk sat in front of the window with white bookshelves on either side of the wall. I'd walked into a Pottery Barn catalogue but still felt the radius of her professional control.

She didn't look up from her computer until I was standing directly in front of her desk. Even when she was sitting, she had perfect posture. Her back didn't touch the chair, and her shoulders were held in precise alignment with her spine. Her hair was loose around her shoulders, soft and long. A slight curl was in the strands, and it made me wonder if her hair was naturally curly. Her makeup was the same was it was last time, subtle and sexy. She rose from her chair, standing in a black dress that was tight and highlighted the perfect contours of her body. With an hourglass frame, she had noticeable tits, a tiny waist, and an ass that was luscious.

She extended her hand to me. "Hunt."

I took it, squeezing her wrist harder than she'd squeezed mine last week. "Titan."

She dropped her hand and sat down again, her legs crossing. Her black stilettos were visible under the desk. Her legs were long and beautiful just like last time. She wore a shiny watch on her wrist and a white gold necklace around her throat. There was a subtle hint of vanilla inside her office, and that's when I noticed the vase of lilies on her table. There were hydrangeas in the lobby. Fresh flowers were a rare sight in corporate offices like this. It seemed like a feminine touch she specifically requested.

"Can I get you something to drink?" She glanced to the shelf on the right side of her office. A liquor cabinet was there, a full wet bar with glasses, a bucket of ice, and fresh fruit. She opened a bottle of whiskey and poured a glass.

I watched her, my eyes entranced by her movements. "I'll have whatever you're having." It was eleven in the morning, and she was already drinking.

Fucking sexy.

"I hope you like Old Fashioneds."

My eyes narrowed with interest. "I do, actually."

She made the drinks and even tossed an orange peel and cherry inside. Her green eyes were locked on mine as she walked across the gray rug and placed the glass on the coffee table beside me. Her heels clapped against the floor with every movement she made, a song that matched her aura perfectly.

I watched her walk around the desk, my eyes focusing on her perfect ass.

It was tight.

She didn't just sit on that ass all day. She hit the gym—at least three times a week. Her arms were toned, and her stomach was as flat as a solid line.

I liked a fit woman. Not just someone who ran every morning, but someone who could pick up a barbell and do twenty squats. I appreciated her physique and wondered how she looked in just her beautiful skin.

She sat down again and took a long drink. When she licked her lips at the end, it almost seemed deliberate.

I drank my own, noting how strong it was. It was definitely a double.

"I don't have much time, Hunt. Get to the point."

The harder she became, the more I admired her. She didn't dance around with bullshit and meaningless words. Everything was clear and concise —just like the rest of her. "Your publishing house has been failing for the past three years. It was never that profitable to begin with, but now it's costing you more to keep the lights on than ever before."

She drank from her glass, finishing half of it without seeming even somewhat affected by the booze. This must be something she did on a regular basis so she'd grown immune to it. She could hold her liquor as well as I could. If I were out with a woman who downed a single one of these, she'd be giddy and right on my lap. "I'm aware of the situation, Mr. Hunt. That doesn't change what I've already said— repeatedly. I'm not interested in selling."

For the richest woman in the world, that didn't seem like a business decision that made sense. "Why?"

"Why doesn't matter."

"It does to me. You seem like a smart woman. You wouldn't be where you are if you owned unsuccessful businesses."

She brought the glass to her lips and finished the rest of it. A lipstick mark now stuck to the glass, a perfect outline of her mouth. I wondered if the same thing would happen if her mouth were pressed against something else. "Why are you so adamant about buying it? You aren't the kind of businessman to reinvent a brand. You start from the ground up. What's your exception in this case?"

I cracked a smile, knowing she'd read up on me. Maybe she Googled me. Maybe she saw the way my life was represented by reporters. Or perhaps she was smart enough to know there was always more to the story. "I think I can turn your publishing house around. I have big plans for it."

She stared me down with her stark green eyes. They were lively like a forest of pine trees, darker more than vibrant. They held profound mystery, a collection of undiscoverable secrets. She displayed very little of her mind, hiding behind her powerful front and absorbing endless information around her. She examined me like a specimen under a microscope, looking at me at an unparalleled magnification. "Diesel Hunt isn't the kind of man to wait for anybody. He's driven, but doesn't chase. He's smart and indifferent. You've attempted to command my attention four times now—to buy a failing publishing house." She leaned forward over her desk, getting a better look at me. She reminded me of a lioness homing in on her prey.

I loved being her prey.

Titan cocked her head to the side, her expression sexy when it was this serious. "Do you want to fuck me?" Her eyes didn't close, not even for a second to blink. She had me cornered so she could watch every little reaction I made.

The skin on the back of my neck immediately prickled, standing on end like a cold draft had entered the office space. My hands rested on the armrests, my fingers gripping the edge of the wood. My cock came to life, unable to resist its natural urgency to grow. The pounding blood left my temples and circled down below, answering the question that my mouth refrained from admitting.

She asked the question with such confidence, looked past my actions and explored the motivations behind them. She didn't arrive at the conclusion because she viewed herself as beautiful. It was simply the most logical explanation for my behavior.

And I found that sexy.

She didn't stop herself from speaking her mind. She said exactly what she thought, regardless of how I would view her. Her eyes shifted back and forth as she examined my face, waiting for the answer she'd already predicted.

I could lie and ignore the way my cock pressed

against my fly in my slacks. But she had agreed to see me on short notice, probably canceled a different meeting to give me an audience. She only would have done that if she was going to get something out of it.

I clenched my jaw hard before I answered because I couldn't remember the last time I was this turned on. She made my spine tighten until it was about to snap in half. All the muscles in my body tensed as the heat flushed through me. Images of me plowing into her right on that desk overcame me. I fucked her mouth, her pussy, and finally finished by coming deep inside her ass.

"Yes."

Her expression didn't change, showing the same hardness as before. She slowly sat back, returning to her stick-straight position behind her desk. She swallowed slightly, the muscles of her neck shifting.

My hands continued to grip the armrests.

When she rose from her desk and walked around, I hoped she was going to straddle my hips and ride me then and there. My cock wanted to be buried deep inside her, to make a home there and never leave.

"As flattered as I am, I don't mix business with pleasure." She leaned against the front of her desk, her hands gripping the white edge.

"Then I won't buy your publishing house. Problem solved." When she gripped her desk the way I gripped my chair, I knew she wanted to feel my hard cock sink inside her. She wouldn't have addressed me so deliberately if she weren't prepared for the answer I gave. She wanted to fuck me too, even if she didn't admit it the way I did.

That diplomatic smile stretched across her lips. "You know what I mean, Hunt."

We both operated in the same stratosphere. We knew the same people. Reporters followed us everywhere we went. She had a bigger reputation to protect than I did. I could fuck every woman in Manhattan, and no one cared. If she simply did her hair wrong, she would get negative headlines.

That was the sad world we lived in.

"I should get back to work. It was nice seeing you, Mr. Hunt." She grabbed my half-full glass from the table and walked back around her desk.

I got another peek of her ass before I rose and walked to the door. Once dismissed, I didn't press my argument. She was right. I didn't want her company that badly. I'd only chased her this far because of my pride. And once I got a good look at her, I only wanted sex. I was willing to buy her company just for the opportunity to fuck her.

That was how much I wanted her.

But she turned me down—again. And she did it so easily.

I glanced over my shoulder before I stepped out.

She had my glass to her lips, and she downed the rest of it, her eyes locked on me. She tipped her head back, getting every single drop and letting the orange peel come into contact with her mouth. When the whiskey was gone, she set the glass on the table. Like last time, she licked her lips.

She licked her lips just for me.

FIVE

Tatum
———————

I DIDN'T WEAR STILETTOS TONIGHT. I WORE
strappy heels that were just as tall as my regular shoes,
and a tight dress that was so tight I could barely
breathe. It was Valentino, so I couldn't care less about
respiration.

Fashion was more important.

Isa and Pilar sat beside me in the circular booth,
both wearing dresses that stopped above their knees.
Heels were on their feet, but they were so used to
wearing them every day for work they didn't think
twice about it.

"How's the runway?" I asked Pilar, who was a
supermodel for one of the biggest brands in the
world. In fact, she was a brand herself.

"Amazing and shitty," she said. "I'm not allowed
to eat this week. Hence, the water." She nodded to

the glass of ice water on the table. "If someone asks me if I'm pregnant one more time…"

I wasn't a big eater, so I'd always been on the slimmer side, but Pilar was all body and no fat. I couldn't cut out the final luxuries I allowed myself in order to have the perfect physique. Being the way I was was enough for me. "Can you eat the lemon?" I teased.

"That's my main course," Pilar said sarcastically.

"Is Thorn coming tonight?" Isa asked.

"No, he's got his own plans." We kept in touch on a daily basis, but we didn't see each other around the clock. We both had our own lives to live.

"Dang," she said. "His friend Bryan is cute."

"I can pass along the message, if you like." Isa was so beautiful it was painful to look at her. I'd already seen a dozen men look our way, their eyes set on her. Pilar was the supermodel, but Isa could easily hit the runway if she wanted to.

"No," she said quickly. "I can always call Thorn if I'm really serious about it."

I preferred to spend my time with ambitious women who had their own goals in mind. If they wanted a guy, they asked him out. If they wanted a raise, they asked for it. Isa had started her own online company that she turned into a million-dollar industry. Instead of blowing away her profits, she reinvested in other things. Now she was a powerful entrepreneur who had every right to be picky about men.

"What's new with you?" Isa asked. "How did that conference go?"

Pilar sipped her water before flicking her hair behind her shoulder. She sat up straight with her shoulders back, diamond earrings in her lobes.

"Well. There were a few assholes reporters, though."

"There always are." Isa rolled her eyes.

"Asked when I was going to have a family," I continued. "Would they have asked Diesel Hunt that question?"

She chuckled. "That guy plows a different girl every night, and society doesn't give a damn about it."

"And then another asked me how it felt to be the richest woman in the world." The questions always got under my skin, but I wasn't allowed to voice my annoyance. The second I fought it, I looked defensive. Pointing out it was sexist just made me appear weak. "Like being a woman made it especially impressive…"

"Men are pigs," Isa said. "If I didn't need that D, I would swear off all of them."

"Me too," Pilar said.

"Then Diesel Hunt offered to buy my publishing company…and wouldn't take no for an answer."

"Diesel Hunt, for real?" Isa asked.

"Dude, he's sooo hot," Pilar said. "If he made a pass at me, I'd be down."

"Like break-your-heart-but-it's-totally-worth-it hot," Isa said. "What did you say?"

"I'm not interested in selling. He tried four separate times to talk to me about it."

Isa raised an eyebrow, the wickedness in her eyes. "Sounds like he's not after the company at all…"

I came to the same conclusion. "It would never work. He's not my type." I had very specific ways of doing things, and I never made an exception. Diesel Hunt didn't fit into my criteria, as hot as he was.

"Not your type?" Isa asked.

"When did hot stop being your type?" Pilar asked.

"I have a reputation to preserve," I reminded them. "Hunt uses women like he uses cars—until they break down and become worthless." Reporters would see us together, the world would talk about us, and then we would go our separate ways. Of course, everyone would assume he left and broke my heart… whether that was the truth or not. Being with a playboy would ruin the aura I'd developed for myself. "He's not worth the trouble."

"Well, you might be right about that," Isa said.

We had more drinks, and eventually, two men joined us. They sat in the booth with Pilar and Isa. One man was between the two of us. It wasn't clear who he was going for—her or me. Maybe he was confident enough to try both of us at the same time.

I excused myself and headed to the bar, not interested in either one of them. I reached the counter and waited less than a second for the bartender to wait on me. There was only one drink I liked in particular, so much that my friends called me Old Fashioned as a nickname. Some of the men at the bar were looking at me, but none of them made a move, either because they recognized me or just assumed I would say no. I didn't make eye contact with anyone, doing my best not to invite them to any kind of interaction.

I didn't pick up men in bars. Too risky.

The bartender set the drink in front of me. "On the house, sweetheart."

I smiled. "Thank you."

"It's not on the house—it's on me." A tall man

VICTORIA QUINN

came to my side and slapped the twenty on the counter. Standing six three and smelling of body soap and cologne stood Diesel Hunt, glorious in his collared shirt and tight slacks. His jaw had just been shaved, and his fair skin was flawless and kissable. His shirt stretched across his shoulders, and his prominent muscles were impossible to ignore. He had thin hips that led to an impressive torso, muscles tied together to form a masterpiece of strength. Tanned skin was visible at the opening of his collar, and it hinted at the gorgeous flesh underneath.

The second he was near, my guard was up. "Thank you for the offer, but that's not necessary."

Diesel kept his eyes on me as he pushed the bill farther across the counter. "Keep the change, man."

The bartender took it without question.

"I had to pay you back for that double you made me last week."

"I drank half of it." Not that he needed me to remind him. "So you don't owe me anything."

He was closer to me than he'd ever been before because the rest of the bar was crammed. He was in my personal space, crossing the line of my invisible bubble. When anyone came too close to me, I automatically stepped back.

Except now.

54

His long and toned legs looked great in his tight slacks. His ass couldn't be seen, but the second he walked away, I would take a peek. Diesel Hunt was America's favorite playboy for a reason. He was packing all the right things. He was good-looking, smart, and extremely charming. Even I wasn't immune.

Hunt finally severed eye contact and turned to the bartender. "I'll have what she's having."

The bartender poured the glass, added the orange peel and cherry, and then slid it toward Hunt.

I slapped a bill on the counter. "That one is on me."

The bartender immediately snatched it and walked off.

Hunt grinned down at me, pleased by my actions rather than annoyed like most men would be. He took the glass and brought it to his lips. "That's hot."

"There's no ice in it?"

He took another drink. "No. Having a woman like you buy me a drink."

"Like me?" I asked.

"Yeah. It's not every day that the richest woman in the world buys me a drink—and the most beautiful."

I couldn't wear my diplomatic smile this time. A laugh escaped, hearty and deep.

Diesel gave me a smile like I'd never seen. "You have a nice laugh. I've never heard it before."

"Most people haven't."

"I'm glad I amuse you—even when I'm being serious." His eyes returned to their harsh seriousness, burning me with their heated stare. They didn't leave my face as he brought the glass to his lips and took another drink. "Yours is better."

"Thank you. I've had a lot of practice."

"You should come to my place and try one of my mine."

When Hunt had walked out of my office, I'd assumed that was the end of his pursuit. But I'd underestimated him. He didn't stop until he got what he wanted. And now, I was his new target. "I already explained my view on the matter."

"But we both know that's not really what you want."

If any other man spoke those words, they would irritate me. But coming from him, a man who made me soak my panties, it was enticing. "It doesn't matter what I want. We're from different worlds—even though we exist in the same one."

Hunt seemed to understand exactly what I was

referring to. He respected me more than the other men I encountered. He didn't attempt to interrupt me or talk over me, and not once did he voice a sexist remark. "Despite what you've read about me, I'm a gentleman. And gentlemen don't kiss and tell."

"Every woman you're with is immediately in the centerfold of every tabloid."

"Because they want to be there. They want their fifteen minutes of fame, fifteen minutes in my bed, and fifteen minutes in my fancy car. But the women who don't want the spotlight never get it. I've been with lots of models and actresses that you don't know about."

"Like whom?"

He wore a quiet smile. "I know you're testing me."

He was right, I was. "And you passed."

He scooted closer to me at the bar, his face now dangerously close to mine. "Come home with me, Titan." When he was this close, his cologne wrapped around me. I got a visual of what it would be like to be in his bed, his powerful body on top of mine as his ass worked to fuck me hard like I enjoyed. "It's just you and me."

"You aren't going to stop until you get what you want, are you?"

All he did was harden his gaze.

That was all the answer I needed. We would have a night of great sex, I would slip out in the morning, and then we would pretend it never happened. That was the perfect setup for me—assuming he was a man who could keep a secret.

His big hand moved to the small of my back, his large fingers taking up most of the area. He gave me a gentle squeeze, bunching up my dress behind me. He positioned me closer to him, his face almost pressed to mine. "Titan, do you want to fuck me?" His eyes focused on my lips, wanting to see the answer and not just hear it.

The attraction was there the second I'd laid eyes on him. I was aroused by his power, his confidence, his relentless determination. I didn't care about his wealth, but I respected his discipline to attain it. I liked a man who stopped at nothing to get what he wanted—even if that very thing was me. He body rippled with tight muscles, and he had a smile that could melt my panties right down my legs.

I stepped closer to him and pressed my lips against the corner of his mouth. It was a soft touch, hardly a kiss, but it was enough to make the warmth flush through my body. It was enough to make my fingertips go numb. "Yes."

HIS PENTHOUSE WAS at the very top of a skyscraper. It had a panoramic view of the city, and everything was touched with dark masculinity. Without knowing the occupant of the house, I would have guessed it belonged to a man of Hunt's description.

Hunt walked to the bar inside his kitchen. "Can I get you a drink?"

I didn't care about having a drink. I unzipped the back of my dress and let it fall into a pile on the floor. Standing in only a black thong and heels, I shot him a fiery look before I helped myself to his bedroom down the hall, knowing he watched me the entire way.

I sat at the edge of the bed and slipped off my heels, knowing he would join me in a matter of seconds.

He made his appearance just as I stood up, now in just the lacy thong that barely covered anything.

He stopped in the doorway and stared at me, his dark eyes lusting over every curve of my body. He took in the sight of my tits, watching my small nipples harden under his dark stare. His gaze sank down my waist to my legs before it moved back up again.

I played with the lace of my panties before I pulled them down my legs.

He watched the entire time.

I scooped up my panties from the ground then approached him, buck naked in his bedroom. My hands went to his belt, and I removed it before I got his slacks loose. When they were open and he was accessible, I wrapped my panties around his length, letting his cock feel how soaked I was.

He breathed against my mouth and gripped my waist with his large hands, his fingers digging into my skin like pressure points. One hand slid to the fall of my hair and cupped the back of my head. His eyes were on my lips, but he didn't kiss me just yet. He drew it out, teasing me.

I'd never wanted to be kissed so badly in my life.

He moved his mouth to mine and kissed me, sending his heated breaths directly into my mouth. The initial touch was soft and slow, both of us gentle as we explored one another for the first time.

Our lips didn't move at all, just pressed together.

And then he kissed me harder, his lips moving against mine with restrained intensity. His fingers moved along the back of my neck as he tightened his grip. His other hand cupped my tits, and he massaged it aggressively, his thumb flicking over my nipple.

Then his tongue came next, diving into my mouth until it met mine.

We kissed, sucked, and licked one another.

My hands moved to his shirt, and I got the buttons loose, revealing lines of muscle and power. He was fit and strong, his pectoral muscles slabs of concrete. His abs were a perfect six-pack, and there were strong lines defining the V of his hips.

My fingertips worshiped his body like it was a shrine.

I moaned into his mouth when I felt the flood of moisture pool between my legs. I was so slick I could take his monster cock with ease. My fingers measured him as I wrapped my panties around his length.

And he was definitely impressive.

My fingers stroked his cock, dragging the inside of my panties down his length. I smeared my own lubrication all over him, making him just as slick as I was.

Now he moaned into my mouth, his cock twitching in my hands. He yanked his shirt off then guided me backward to the bed. The backs of my knees hit the mattress, forcing me to sit down.

Hunt pulled his boxers down, my panties dropping with him.

He was so sexy.

He was six foot three of pure sex, pure fantasy. Tanned skin was tight across his powerful body. He was strong in all the right places, and soft nowhere the eye could see. He had a tight and muscular ass and a torso that could break down a brick wall. His dark hair was perfectly styled because my fingers hadn't destroyed it—yet.

His cock was the most impressive feature, nine inches and noticeably thick. He let me stare at it, obviously proud of the tool he was about to fuck me with.

I licked my lips, deeply impressed.

His eyes narrowed in hunger, and he ripped open a foil packet and rolled a condom onto his length.

Finally, the best part.

We moved to the head of the bed, and he positioned himself on top of me, obviously wanting to fuck me exactly the way I was. His massive body forced mine to sink into the bed, the pillows surrounding me because his weight was heavy. I parted my knees so his hips could fit between my thighs. I wanted to give this man plenty of room, knowing he was going to rock me just the way I wanted.

He held his head above mine and rubbed his cock

against my folds. "How do you want me to fuck you? Slow and deep—"

"I want it hard." I grabbed his hips and pulled him toward me, sliding the head of his cock inside me. The second I felt him, I moaned, my mind deliriously happy with this beautiful man on top of me.

Diesel widened my legs farther and thrust himself hard inside me, giving me all nine inches immediately. The headboard smacked against the wall at the motion because there was so much force in the movement.

"Yes..." My nails tested his skin, feeling the softness I wanted to slice through. My ankles locked together around his lower back, and I gripped his shoulders as an anchor. I used the muscles of my arms and back to move him inside me, to sheathe his fat cock over and over.

Hunt watched me, excitement flaring in his eyes. He adjusted his arms before he started to move, fucking me hard just the way I asked. He fucked me so hard the wooden headboard would definitely leave a mark in the wall.

He grunted and breathed, using his tight ass to bury his desire between my legs. The slick sounds our adjoined bodies made caused both of us to groan in pleasure more than once. My legs widened to give him more room, feeling his enormous body work hard to fuck me the way I asked.

I was gonna come.

And not just come like a normal person.

But fucking explode.

"Hunt...you're gonna make me come."

He gripped the back of my hair and kept me firmly in place as he smacked into me, his balls slapping against my ass. Every inch of his big length hit me over and over again. He looked me in the eye, fiery and aggressive.

I came with a scream, my entire body tightening as his cock did amazing things to me. My nipples hardened into diamonds, and I dragged my nails down his back as he brought me into home plate. I gushed all over his cock, my cream sheathing him all the way to the balls. "Hunt..."

He was about to come. I could see the desire building up in his eyes. It was only a matter of seconds before he filled the tip of the condom.

I rolled him onto his back and straddled him without pulling him out of me. I balanced on the balls of my feet and pressed my hands against his chest. I lowered myself over and over, taking his big cock without breaking my stride. My thighs ached and my ass was tight, but that didn't slow me down.

Hunt moved underneath me, thrust his hips up so he could fuck me even faster than he did before. We moved together at lightning speed, fucking like animals that hadn't been ravaged like this in all our lives.

"Come," I commanded, working so fast my tits were shaking up and down. Sweat coated my body, and my hands nearly slipped against his chest. It was so much work, but damn, it felt so good.

He grabbed my hips and pulled me hard against him, shoving all of his cock inside me as he came. A masculine groan escaped his lips, filling his bedroom and my ears. He twitched inside me, come filling the tip of the condom as his cock was lodged deep inside me. "Fuck…Titan." He closed his eyes for a brief second as he recovered from the scorching orgasm that nearly killed both of us.

It was good, even better than I expected. Hunt knew how to fuck just like he knew how to make money. His cock was humungous, exactly what I wanted in a partner. He had the tools that could fix my engine anytime.

I pulled off him and lay beside him, catching my breath now that I was sweaty and warm. I eyed the tip of the condom and saw all the come he'd released for me. There was tons. I would have struggled to swallow it if I'd been on my knees, sucking his cock. I was satisfied, but a part of me wished that come were sitting deep inside me.

It was one of my kinks.

Hunt was quiet as he caught his breath beside me. He eventually closed his eyes, and when his breathing changed, I knew he'd slipped into sleep.

That's when I got dressed and left.

SIX

Hunt

WHEN I WOKE UP THE FOLLOWING MORNING, SHE was gone.

No note.

Nothing. Nada. Zip.

That woman didn't mess around, did she?

Every woman I'd taken back to my place had stayed until the following morning. Most of them, even longer than that. And it even got to the point where I had to offer to give them a ride home because they weren't getting the hint.

But she must have left the second I pulled out of her.

She was like a man—but as a woman.

My week passed with its usual chaos. There was too much to do and not enough hours in the day. Even if I worked around the clock, I still wouldn't be able to manage everything. With executives managing places I never physically visited, I still wasn't covering enough ground.

But to a man like me, even everything wasn't enough.

I got lost in my work enough that I stopped thinking about the woman I'd taken back to my apartment. But like a sinister thought that just wouldn't go away, she haunted me. She popped back into my brain at the strangest times, even in the middle of a meeting.

I didn't tell my friends about her, keeping my word to Titan. She didn't want anyone to know about us, to avoid the public obsession that followed me everywhere I went, and I respected her request.

I was a gentleman, after all.

And I made her come like every gentleman should.

But I'd expected her to call my office or get a hold of my phone number. I'd left a business card with her assistant so she would know how to reach me. But I didn't hear a peep out of her.

It was like that night never happened.

I should be happy. That's exactly how I liked most of my affairs—with a clean break. As soon as I shut the door, I never wanted to see that woman again. I didn't want her to blow up my phone asking for another date.

But now that all I had was silence, I second-guessed my preferences.

I thought being with her once would satisfy me enough to stop thinking about her.

But fuck, I wanted her more.

What the hell?

Was it because the sex was that good? Or was it just because she didn't give a damn whether I lived or died?

Beats me.

There was an opening to a new club downtown that I received an invite to. I was planning on going with the guys to spend money, hook up with women, and talk shit about any competition we had.

And I wondered if she would be there.

She had been at Atlas, which had the same owner as this new place.

My chances were good. I would meet with her again naturally and see where things went. If she weren't there, then I'd have to figure out another plan.

———

THE SOUND of the bass drowned out most of the conversation. Pine and Mike both had a girl under their arms in the booth. One of the women's friends sat next to me, but I didn't make a pass. She was pretty, of course, but my mind was elsewhere.

My eyes were glued to the entrance.

We got there late, on purpose. We never showed up to anything until the last minute, and of course, there was always a table waiting for us. My eyes glanced to a group of women that walked inside, but none of them was Titan.

Pine waved his hand in front of my face. "Who are you looking for? You've got a perfect ten right here." He pointed his thumb at the nameless blonde beside me.

I didn't answer him, my eyes still on the entryway.

"I bet he's looking for Titan," Mike commented.

"You're still on her?" Pine asked incredulously. "She's hot but seems uptight."

"She's not uptight." I couldn't diminish the anger in my tone. He hit a trigger I didn't know I had.

Pine raised both hands when he realized he'd pissed me off. "Fine…she's not uptight. You are."

That insult was okay—if it was meant for me. Because I was the most uptight guy on the planet.

"Anything more happen with her?" Pine asked.

I told my friends everything. We'd been through a lot together, a lot of ups and downs. It was felt strange not telling them the truth when they asked me a direct question, but I had to protect her reputation. "No."

"Then you're never going to seal the deal," Pine said.

"She's with Thorn Cutler anyway," Mike said. "They've been on and off since I can remember."

My head snapped in his direction so hard I almost pulled a tendon. "What?"

"Thorn Cutler," Mike repeated. "You know him."

I'd heard of the guy, but I didn't care about that. "She's seeing him?"

Mike shrugged. "That's what I heard. It doesn't seem like it's ever been confirmed or denied because their relationship is pretty secretive, but they're spotted together all the time."

She had a boyfriend?

Did she cheat on him with me?

My blood boiled at the thought, disgusted that any human being would do such a deceitful thing. But when I thought about her character, her obvious concern about the world's perception of her, that didn't make sense. There must be some kind of explanation.

I'd give her the benefit of the doubt.

"Speaking of the devil…" Pine nodded to the entryway.

Titan walked inside with Thorn Cutler right beside her. They didn't hold hands or show any affection, but they were close to each other, closer than two friends would stand together. The two girls I saw her with last time came up behind her. One was a supermodel, and another was a fellow business owner. She kept a tight circle just the way I did.

They sat at a table that had obviously been reserved for them. Thorn ordered their drinks, getting her an Old Fashioned like she liked, and they talked amongst themselves. Laughs were exchanged, and smiles were plastered on the faces.

Thorn and Titan were close together, their shoulders touching. Thorn looked into the crowd, more preoccupied with seeing who else was there than paying attention to her.

I found that odd.

When I stared longer than I should, I looked away. I didn't know what my next move was. Thorn complicated matters. It was none of my business if she was sleeping with him or not, but I wanted to know anyway.

———

I ENTERTAINED myself watching them together on the dance floor. The girls moved to the music, and it wasn't long before men joined them, doing their best to get as close as possible. One guy grabbed Titan's hand and spun her around.

She went with it.

My eyes immediately went to Thorn.

He watched them before he pulled out his phone and texted someone.

He didn't give a damn—at all.

Now I was even more suspicious than before. If Titan were my woman, I wouldn't let her dance with some guy while I busied myself on my phone.

They kept moving with the music, and when his hand slid around her waist something inside me snapped.

I got out of my seat, walked onto the dance floor, and took her for myself.

What the hell was I doing?

I spun her around and pulled her into my chest, dancing with her like I'd been there the whole time.

The look Titan gave me was a mix of horror and utter surprise. She faltered in her moves before she picked up the beat again.

I stared the guy down, telling him to back off if he wanted his head to stay on his shoulders.

He made the right decision and walked away.

I pulled her close to me and danced with her, our eyes locked together just the way they were when we fucked in my bed just a week ago. I remembered exactly how it felt to be between her legs. My cock was rock-hard and about to burst every second I was buried between her legs. The sound of her orgasm would be permanently embedded in my mind for the rest of time, along with the face she made when she came around my dick.

Her friends finished the song and walked away with their dates, hitting the bar to rehydrate. I grabbed her by the hand and pulled her off the dance floor, away from her friends and mine.

She didn't pull away like I thought she might.

When we were in the darkness away from everyone, I finally spoke my mind. "It's been a while, Titan."

"I suppose." She adjusted her hair with her fingertips, taming the wild strands after hitting the dance floor. She wore a sleeveless burgundy dress, a nice color for her skin tone. She wore diamond earrings that were worth more than most people's cars. The necklace around her throat looked ten times as expensive. She didn't lavish herself with jewels, but she definitely wore classy pieces to highlight her stature.

I was floored when she acted like nothing had happened between us. If she'd spotted me first, she probably wouldn't have stopped by to say hello. I shouldn't be surprised, and I certainly shouldn't care, but that wasn't going to happen. "I heard you and Thorn are a bit of an item." I didn't directly ask her the question, seeing how she would react to the speculation.

She met my gaze fearlessly, saying nothing.

I kept my silence, not backing down.

She didn't back down either.

Jesus, she was stubborn. "You don't have a comment to that?"

"I don't kiss and tell."

I cocked my head, annoyed by her feistiness.

"My personal life is none of your concern, Hunt."

"It's not?" I asked. "Because you just fucked me last week."

"Your point?" she asked coldly. "So a man can sleep around, but a woman can't?"

"Are you sleeping around?"

She crossed her arms over her chest. "What is this

about, Hunt? Did you really come over here to interrogate me? You strike me as a man who doesn't care if a woman he slept with one time is sleeping with someone else."

When she put it that way, it seemed like I was overreacting. "I'm not a big fan of cheating."

"Me neither."

If that was her response, I suppose I had nothing to worry about. It explained why he didn't care if she pressed up against some guy on the dance floor. It explained why he was more invested in his phone than her whereabouts.

Titan held my gaze a little longer before she glanced over her shoulder. "I should be getting back. It was nice seeing you, Hunt." She turned away.

I grabbed her and pulled her back toward me. Just when she opened her mouth to tell me off, I guided her against the wall and kissed her. My hand fisted her soft hair, and I enveloped her in the shadows. Once my mouth was on hers, she kissed me back immediately. There was no hesitation on her part.

She wanted me.

I ground against her, the music playing over the speakers and loud conversations surrounding us. My cock was hard, and I pressed that against her stomach, wanting her to know I wanted her as much now as I did the other night. Our mouths devoured each other, and our tongues swirled together, dancing erotically.

My hand snaked under her dress, and my fingers dug inside her underwear. The second I touched her folds, I noticed her wetness.

She was soaked.

She definitely wanted me.

I kept my mouth against hers but ended the kiss. "Come to my place."

Her eyes left my lips and met my gaze. "That was a one-time thing, Hunt."

"Your wet panties say otherwise."

She narrowed her eyes in anger, but the rest of her body came alive with an electric current. Her pulse increased, and her breathing went haywire. Her normally pale cheeks were flushed with redness. "No."

"Yes."

Her cheeks flushed more when I refused to accept her answer.

I ground my cock right against her clit, rubbing against that nub the way all women loved.

She released an involuntary moan.

My mouth found her ear. "No man can make you come the way I do."

Her arms reluctantly circled my neck, and she breathed directly into my ear.

"Now come home with me."

———

I WAS on my knees and positioned behind her, pounding my enormous cock inside her unbelievably tight pussy. Even through a condom, I could feel how wet she was. White globs of cream sheathed the condom because she kept coming all over my dick.

Her screams were muffled when she pressed her face into the sheets. Her panties were around her ankles, and her dress hiked up so I could fuck her. I didn't even get my shirt off before we got down to business.

My hands were on her hips, and she gripped my wrists as she held on, our bodies moving together in slick unison. Her ass was in the air, that beautiful asshole looking back at me. Her body was beautiful, flawless and sexy. I loved to drag my tongue across her skin, tasting her and marking her at the same time.

She came again, her pussy full of my cock. "Hunt..."

I closed my eyes for a heartbeat, savoring the sound of my name. I'd never enjoyed making a woman come so much in my life. Making her come was enough for me to let go, but I made her come three times before I allowed myself to release.

I fucked her like I had something to prove.

I fucked her like I didn't want her to forget me.

I fucked her so she would be there in the morning.

When I was ready to explode, I pulled out of her, ripped the condom off, and came all over her ass. I wanted my heavy come to touch her directly, to claim her in a way other men couldn't. I jerked myself hard until every single drop landed on her luscious skin. A final moan escaped my lips when I finished.

She remained on the bed with her face in the sheets, just as exhausted as I was.

I cleaned myself off in the bathroom and disposed of the condom. The nice thing to do would be to get her toilet paper to clean herself off, but I wanted her to do it herself. I wanted her to feel how much come I'd sprayed all over her.

When she walked into the bathroom, she checked her reflection in the mirror.

And she saw it.

Her eyes contracted in arousal. The reaction was short, but I caught it.

And I grinned.

She came back into the bedroom and found her panties on the ground.

I tapped the area next to me on the bed, silently commanding her to lay beside me.

She eyed the spot before she pulled on her panties and adjusted her dress.

Did she ever follow directions? "Titan." I patted the spot beside me again, making the sheets puff under my touch.

She dismissed my invitation. "I should get going…" She turned away to grab her shoes.

That's when I hooked my arm around her waist and yanked her onto the bed. She crashed against my chest when we were both in the center of the mattress. "Does everything need to be straight business with you?"

"When it's a business matter, yes." She propped herself up on her elbow and looked down at me. When her hair was messy like that and her mascara was smeared, she looked even sexier. She looked like a very handsome man had just fucked her good and hard. Her lips were swollen, and her lipstick had disappeared—because it was somewhere on my body.

I rested my head back on the pillow and watched her with a perfect view. Her long body stretched out across the bed, and I saw the way her torso led to a narrow waist. I preferred her naked, but she was still sexy in that skintight fabric.

Her hand moved to my stomach, and she slowly slid her hand over my six-pack, her fingers gliding over the tough grooves of my muscles. Her soft fingers were a direct contrast to my hardness. It was like rubbing a feather against sandpaper. Her eyes darkened imperceptibly, but the reaction was enough to tell me she enjoyed the touch.

I was glad she liked touching me as much as I liked touching her.

She turned her head until her eyes landed on mine. She examined my messy hair before she stared my lips. "You're a very handsome man." Her hand slid to my chest, feeling the hard muscles of my pectorals.

Titan wasn't the kind of person who handed out compliments, and if she did, it was because you earned them. "Thank you."

Her hand snaked down again, her fingertips drawing lines across my skin until she reached my happy trail. She felt the scruff before she circled back up again. "And your place is nice too."

"Maybe I can see yours sometime." The words popped into my brain just a millisecond before I spoke them out loud. As a successful man, I always considered everything I said in detail before I let another human being listen to my words. But with Titan, there wasn't much thinking going on.

Just doing.

Her hand continued to explore my body, her eyes not giving the slightest reaction to what I said.

What was she thinking?

"I hope your girlfriends aren't worried about you."

"They know I can handle myself." She had an answer for everything, like she'd already witnessed this conversation and rehearsed what to say. Not once had I seen her flustered. Even when faced with difficult questions, she cruised through them without fumbling. She was the world's most graceful woman —not just the richest. "And they can handle themselves."

"Do they know about me?"

"What is there to tell?"

I propped myself up on my elbow so we were eye-to-eye. Even when I turned my body, her palm remained glued to my muscular torso. She could act indifferent to me all she wanted, but her affection was unmistakable. "That I don't just make you come hard —but good."

When she smiled, she didn't project that diplomatic grin that she reserved for her adversaries. Now there was a gentle smile on her mouth, a soft affection in her eyes. Her hand moved up my chest and neck until her fingers were right against my jaw. She felt the scruff that had grown in since that morning. The hair was dark and rough where she explored my short beard. "I haven't told them about you—but I will."

"Sounds like you trust your friends."

"Of course I do. They're my family."

I didn't know anything about her family. All I knew was she was insanely rich, classy, and smart. But now I'd have to do some digging—especially into Thorn Cutler. "Will you tell Thorn about me?"

Her smile didn't fade away. "For a man who's just interested in getting laid, you ask a lot of questions."

"Who said I was only interested in getting laid?"

She sized me up with those watchful eyes. "Well, that's all I'm interested in. I hope the same from you."

Every woman I'd been with wanted more. If I

asked them to stay, they would. If I asked them to quit their job and run off with me to Greece, they would. I'd never met a woman so detached, so indifferent. It was definitely a new experience. "I have an open mind."

"I don't." She sat up and fixed her hair before she moved to the edge of the bed. "Thank you for the fun evening."

I didn't want her to leave, but I'd already asked her to stay once. I couldn't do it again. "You know where to find me if you have an itch you just can't scratch."

She slipped on her heels then stood up. "I'll keep that in mind."

I wasn't sure why I expected tonight to be different from the last one. She only saw me as a fuck machine, a man to make her come on cue. And that was perfect for me, more than perfect. I fucked her once to my satisfaction. Now I'd fucked her again, and I was ready to move on.

Or was I?

I got dressed and walked her to the door. "Can I take you home?"

"No, thank you." She grabbed her clutch from where she left it in the entryway. Her hair was fixed, and it didn't seem like she'd just gotten fucked—

minus the missing lipstick. "Goodbye, Hunt." Her hand glided up my bare chest, and she kissed me on the mouth, soft and lovely.

That mouth was perfect. I kissed her back and nibbled on her bottom lip slightly, pulling out a quiet sigh from her slender throat. I took her breath away, and we both knew it. Her bones ached for my touch, for my kiss. I proved it tonight at that club. Once I pressed my body against hers, she was mine.

And she would be mine again. "Good night, Titan."

Her hand slid down my chest as she walked away, her long nails gently scratching me during their departure. Her ass shook as she walked, her perky behind just as sexy in the dress as it was bare. Her heels tapped against the hardwood floor as she walked off, the graceful sound announcing her departure.

I stared at her as she got into the elevator and turned around. I was just in my slacks with bare feet. My hard body was still flexed with the adrenaline that she generated with her touch. I examined her intimately, watching every feature of her face. When I stared too long at a woman, she eventually looked down. The heat became too much.

But Titan wasn't a woman who looked away.

She held my gaze, refusing to be intimidated by any man—not even me.

Our gazes locked, the elevator beeped, and the doors slowly began to close.

As they slid together toward the center, her profile became less visible. Her body faded away until I could only see an inch of her.

Then the doors closed.

Neither one of us won the standoff.

But neither one of us lost either.

SEVEN

Tatum

———————

No man could fuck like Hunt.

Jesus Christ, he was a machine.

I hadn't had sex that exquisite in a while, not that my sex life was ever boring. His cock was big, and he certainly knew how to use it. His kisses were scorching, his touch was tantalizing, and he knew exactly how to work a clitoris.

I was actually sore, but I liked it.

I didn't sleep over at a man's house—not when it was casual. I always got out of there before things could get complicated. I didn't have time for complicated.

Or anything else.

Hunt seemed like the kind of man who didn't want anything serious either. From what I'd researched about him, he was the kind of man who usually traveled with two women, one on each arm. He was never photographed with the same woman more than once, and he was hailed as a sex symbol other men looked up to. He definitely wasn't a man who would have a wife and kids someday.

Perfect for me.

But our arrangement had to end now. I already broke my one-time rule because he ruthlessly seduced me. But it couldn't happen again—not ever. We had a great time, but now we needed to forget about each other and move on.

No matter how hot he was.

A few days passed, and I didn't hear from Hunt. I assumed that meant he'd moved on just the way I did, but I'd be lying if I said I didn't think about that toned physique and those powerful arms. His shoulders were sexy, so broad and strong. Everything about him was innately man, the finest male specimen on the planet. When he was plowing his hard cock inside me, I felt like a woman—and only a woman. I wasn't a CEO, a role model, or a ruthless businesswoman.

I was just a woman.

It was nice.

I even played with my vibrator while thinking about him a few times that week.

But that memory would fade in time. My attraction would die when I found my next partner. He would go back to being a business associate I seldom interacted with. That was perfect for me.

I was in my office when my cell phone rang, and Isa's name appeared on the screen. No one else could reach me directly besides my closest friends and business associates. Everyone else had to go through my four assistants—and even then, it was tough to get through to me. "Hey."

"Hey, how's it going over there?"

"Good. Just got out of a meeting five minutes ago."

"Ugh, I hate meetings. I feel like we sit around and talk but don't get anything done."

I put her on speakerphone so I could sort through my emails at the same time. "I know what you mean."

After a pregnant pause, she addressed the real reason why she was calling me. "So...you disappeared the other night. Where'd you run off to?"

I hadn't told her about Hunt. I was going to, but I assumed I would do it while Pilar was around. "Snuck off with a guy."

"Ooh...what guy?"

"A very hot guy."

VICTORIA QUINN

"Tell me everything."

"Well…you remember Diesel Hunt, right?"

After a long pause, she nearly let out a scream. "You did not."

"I did…"

"How was he?"

A shiver went up my spine just thinking about it. "Unbelievable."

"I'm so jealous right now."

"Every woman should be jealous, honestly. Three times."

"He fucked you three times? Or made you come three times?"

I grinned. "Both."

"Ooh…that sounds amazing."

"And it wasn't my first time. We hooked up two weeks ago too."

Now the pause she gave me was full of a million other feelings. "You slept with him twice?"

"Yeah."

"You?"

"Uh-huh."

"Tatum Titan?"

"Yes, that's me."

"What does that mean?" she asked. "Do you actually like him?"

I respected him, which was saying something coming from me. I enjoyed those kisses and caresses. But my feelings toward him didn't exist out of the physical spectrum. "Not romantically. I told him it wouldn't happen again."

"And he was fine with that?"

"He's such a manwhore. Yes, he was fine with it."

"What did Thorn have to say about it?"

"Haven't talked to him yet."

"You guys are stuck together like glue. I'm surprised."

"We're having dinner tonight. I'll give him the rundown then. Anything happen with you that night?"

"Well…"

I ignored my emails and focused all my attention on our conversation. "Well, what? Who did you take home?"

"Pine Rosenthal."

I didn't recognize the name. "Not sure who that is."

"His family owns a lot of banks. He's wealthy by birth."

Most wealthy people were. "You like him?"

"He's great in bed. Yes, I like him."

"Are you gonna see him again?"

"I hope so," she said. "But I'm playing it cool right now."

"Good. Always make them work for it."

Isa pulled the phone away so she could speak to her assistant. They shared a few words before she came back to me. "Girl, I gotta go."

"Talk to you later." I hung up then noticed a new email in my inbox.

From Diesel Hunt.

MS. TITAN,

I'm taking you to lunch in fifteen minutes.

See you then.

A.

———

WHAT THE HELL was going on? Why did Diesel think he had the privilege to walk into my office whenever he felt like it? Our last conversation had a ring of finality to it, telling me we would never see each other on purpose again.

So what was he doing?

I glanced through the glass doors of my office and saw a tall figure in a dark suit. I recognized those broad shoulders because I'd gripped them several times. My nails remembered his tough skin as I'd nearly sliced him until he bled. That dark hair was perfectly styled, and my fingertips went numb at the thought of ruffling it while he pounded into me in bed.

Jessica's voice sounded over the intercom a moment later. "Titan, Diesel Hunt is here to see you. He says he has a lunch meeting with you, although I don't see it on the schedule."

Because it wasn't on the schedule. "Thank you, Jessica." I didn't let my irritation escape in my voice. "Send him in." When I released the button, I realized how hard I'd been pressing it down. My joint actually ached.

Hunt let himself inside, infecting my space with compelling masculinity like it was his own office. One hand placed inside his pocket, he walked to my desk with a kingly air. A smile was in his eyes, telling me he knew this would tick me off, but it amused him nonetheless. "Ms. Titan."

"Titan, please."

He gave a curt nod before he sat down. His long legs stretched out before him, his muscular thighs noticeable through his slacks. Now that I'd seen him naked, I knew exactly why his clothes hugged him in such perfect ways. I understood why his suit stretched across his broad shoulders—because his body was pure perfection.

He made himself right at home, his powerful persona permeating the air so I was forced to breathe it in. He commanded an entire room with his silence, naturally exuding the kind of strength that men like Julius Caesar could never attain.

I stared him down with my legs crossed underneath my desk. If anyone else pulled this stunt, I'd give him a piece of my mind and rip his balls from between his legs. But Hunt was different. Somehow, he sheathed my anger with his handsomeness. "Can I help you, Hunt?"

"Where do you want to go for lunch?"

"I already ate."

"Liar."

My eyes narrowed at the accusation.

"What?" he asked with a smile. "I like to call people out on their bullshit."

"What a coincidence. So do I."

That charming grin stayed put.

"I'm very busy, so don't waste any more of my time. What do you want?"

He cocked his head slightly to the side, the intensity of his gaze never fading away. He looked at me in the exact same way he did when I stood in his elevator. His stare was intrusive, as if he could see me naked even when I was fully clothed. "You."

"You can't have me." No man ever could. Hunt wouldn't be any different.

"I think otherwise. I'd prove it to you if your doors weren't made of glass."

Cocky bastard.

"Or I will anyway, if you don't mind."

My thighs gave an involuntary squeeze, affected by this man's arrogance as much as I was by his sexiness. "I'm not interested in a relationship with you, Hunt. And if I'm not mistaken, you don't seem like a man interested in a relationship with me either." He preferred to plow different women every night, fucking one while another patiently waited for her turn like a dog. His profound masculinity and his paramount levels of testosterone were both innately desirable to me—but only temporarily.

"We're of one mind, Titan," he said. "But I still want you."

"I don't want you."

He grinned wider than before, his arrogance shining in his eyes. "Bullshit."

My thighs squeezed together again. "I don't want to be associated with you, Hunt."

"Why not?"

"I already told you why."

"No one has to know. I'm a gentleman that can keep a secret."

Keeping a secret was of the least importance. "To be plain, you aren't what I'm looking for."

"Really?" he asked, cocking his head further. "Then what are you looking for?"

Like I could ever tell him. "It doesn't matter."

"It does matter." His jaw was cleanly shaven, his shadow not visible this early in the day. "Because I can give you exactly what you're looking for."

Unlikely. "I don't think so."

"Try me."

Like I could ever let that secret get out. I trusted Hunt not to tell anyone he fucked me, but I didn't trust him not to tell the world about…my fetishes. "Hunt, I'm only going to say this once. Whatever we had is over."

"When you stop squeezing your thighs together, I'll believe you."

How did he know? The desk was between us, so he couldn't see. Unless he was calling my bluff.

"I want you, Titan." He leaned forward, resting his elbows on his knees. "We fuck well together. We fuck like a man and a woman should fuck. I want to keep doing it—and so do you."

That was true, with a few kinks. "I think you just hate being told no."

"I'm a grown man—not a child. I've proven that many times now."

"Then you're just an arrogant asshole who won't stop until he gets what he wants."

He rose to his feet and approached my desk, his height creating a large shadow over the surface even though there was sunlight coming through my window. His large hands pressed against the white wood of my table, calling me to complete attention. "Yes, I'm used to always getting my way. But the only reason why I'm here is because I want you—not because you won't let me have you."

For just a brief second, I wanted to crumble and tell him the truth. I wanted to tell him about every dark secret I had, about the fiery things that consumed me. I wanted to tell him exactly how to touch me, exactly how to fuck me.

But rational thought set in once more. "I have a busy schedule ahead of me, Hunt. Please show yourself out." Just like in thousands of meetings I'd had in my lifetime, I kept my voice steady no matter how hostile the client was. I looked him in the eye, my hands resting calmly on the desk.

Hunt didn't flinch, his potent masculinity filling the air between us. "Goodbye, Titan." He finally stepped back, taking his long and muscular arms away from me and my furniture. The tight muscles of his arms could easily shatter my beautiful desk into pieces if he snapped. His brown eyes locked on to mine, full of authority. "For now."

————

I WALKED into the restaurant and found Thorn sitting at our usual table. He was in a dark blue suit and tie, shiny black shoes on his feet. A white gold watch sat on his wrist, the jewelry worth more than the restaurant. He was on his phone, but he quickly slid it into his pocket once he noticed me approach the table.

He rose to his feet, towering over me by feet, not inches. His arm slid around my waist, and he pressed a kiss to my cheek. "Hey, Old Fashioned." He pulled out my chair for me and helped me sit down before he took his seat again.

"Sorry I'm late. Got held up at the office."

"No worries. Just gave me more time to drink."

He held up his wineglass, which contained a deep red liquid. He swirled it before he brought it to his lips, returning to his somber mood. Anytime we were in a crowd of people, he had walls erected so high you could barely see the sky. "Wine?"

"Sure."

He poured me a glass before he rested his elbows on the table, his blue eyes on me. "Bruce Carol is doing worse. From what I hear, he's gonna take this to the public, probably an auction."

My body tightened, like it did anytime I heard of an obvious opportunity. "When?"

"Soon. We'll have to make our move."

Thorn and I were the kind of business adversaries you didn't want to mess with. We were only loyal to each other, enemies of anyone else outside our group. Neither one of us had weaknesses, only strengths. Combined together, we were a terrifying powerhouse. "I think we can flip that business pretty easily. With my marketing background with the agency, I know how to put his product on the map."

"I was thinking the same thing." His fingers wrapped around the stem of his glass. "He won't settle easily, even though he's desperate. Losing his business to a woman will only get under his skin. It's a backhanded insult."

One of the things I liked about Thorn was his fierce honesty. He didn't buffer the blow. He didn't twist reality to make it easier for me to hear. Sexism was a huge obstacle in my universe, and Thorn chose not to pretend it didn't exist.

One of the reasons why I loved him. "True."

"So, we lowball him, of course. But if he doesn't bite, we'll have to offer him something better. I was thinking ten percent royalties."

"Ten percent." I cocked an eyebrow, annoyed Thorn even made the suggestion. "I don't hand out stakes in my company."

"It's not a stake. It's short term."

"How short?"

"One year. He may despise you because of your tight skirt, but he can't ignore your credentials. He knows he'll make some cash, probably most of what he lost. He won't turn it down. I think it's the final weapon in our arsenal."

It was a good backup plan since it was temporary. Thorn didn't even have access to any ownership of my company—for the moment. "Let's proceed."

"Have your staff set up the meeting. I know you can handle this one on your own."

Thorn and I were never seen doing business together. Everything was behind the scenes. People speculated on what kind of relationship we had, and their assumptions were never right.

That was a good thing.

"I'll let you know when the meeting is scheduled."

"Perfect."

When the waiter came over, Thorn ordered for the both of us. He knew I would order a salad—because that was all I ever ordered. He ordered the same thing but added tender strips of steak on top. A basket of bread was dropped on the table, but neither one of us touched it.

Thorn finished his glass then refilled it. "Who did you take home the other night?"

He broached the exact topic I wanted to discuss. "Funny story, actually."

"I doubt I'll laugh."

People insisted Thorn Cutler was hard and cruel, a ruthless entrepreneur who only cared about money. That wasn't entirely true. He had a heart he was ashamed to show—after having it broken so many times. "Diesel Hunt."

Thorn kept his fingers on the stem of his glass as his eyes narrowed on my face. His eyebrow ridges pressed forward, giving him a slight scowl that interrupted his handsome features. "So he wasn't interested in your business, after all."

"I'm still not sure about that."

"How was he?"

"Like you wouldn't believe…" I swirled my wine before I took a drink. My deep red lipstick left a perfect stain against the glass. The last place my lips had been was on Hunt's skin. I remembered how warm and hard his body had felt underneath my fingertips. I wanted to slice him just to feel his strength. "He was so good that I slept with him twice."

Thorn's interest evaporated like hot steam. "Tay, you need to be careful."

Very few people called me that. If anyone tried without my permission, they regretted it. "It's over."

"Is it really?"

"Yes." Hunt stormed into my office and made me squirm in my chair, but I didn't let him win. I won the battle, and he left the war.

"I don't know much about him other than he's a manwhore. But aren't we all?" Thorn's eyebrows furrowed, but a smile formed on his lips. "I can't tell what kind of man he is other than that."

"He said he was a gentleman, the kind that didn't kiss and tell."

Thorn's shoulders relaxed. "Good. He's probably done with you and ready to move on anyway."

That had yet to be determined. "Yeah…"

"Did he ask about me?"

"Yes." He questioned me with a touch of jealousy.

"And what did you say?"

"Nothing."

"Nothing?" he asked, cocking his head.

"I deflected, told him my personal life was none of his business."

"But he thinks we're an item?"

After our conversation in the corner of the club, I wasn't sure where his head was on that topic. We'd gone to his place and fucked like animals. "I'm not sure what he thinks. If he does think we're together, he doesn't seem to care too much."

"That's perfect. I never hear anything about him in the media, so he seems like a man who keeps his personal life under wraps. He's probably fine. Doesn't seem like a talker."

I hardly knew Hunt, but I felt like I'd known him for a long time. I could speak to his character without knowing any details. I could speak of his loyalty without ever experiencing it. I could speak of his commitment without seeing him pursue anything in his life. "He wouldn't betray me. He's a good man."

Thorn was about to take a sip his wine, but he

steadied himself and looked at me instead. "Titan." All he said was my name, but he said so much more than that. "A good man?"

I drank my wine, as poised as ever.

"I'm starting to think you actually like this guy."

"I don't. I just know he's different from the others."

"Different, huh? Are you going to ask him to be yours?"

I'd be lying if I said I hadn't thought about it. "No. He doesn't fit the bill."

"How so?"

"He's too dominant. He would never give me any power over him." It was one of the reasons my legs could hardly stay together. He had the kind of power I craved, the kind of authority that made me want to obey. Nothing got me hotter than unbridled strength, and the fact that this man had it made me want him even more. But it also made me avoid him like the plague, knowing I could never let him control me.

Thorn gave a slight nod. "True. He doesn't seem like the kind of man who would get on his knees."

"No." He definitely wasn't.

"At least you had your fun with him. Now you can move on."

These lustful feelings would expire, just as they

had for others in the past. Right now, he was a heavy fog in my mind. Anytime I wasn't focusing on a task, I was thinking about him. And when my eyes were closed and I was lying in the dark of my bedroom, my hand had a mind of its own. His deep chocolate eyes looked into mine, pulsing and terrifying. He stripped me naked with just their stare, their power seeping into my veins like a needle releasing its drug. "Yeah…now I can move on."

EIGHT

Hunt

─────────

TATUM TITAN.

A real piece of work.

She was stubborn, ruthless, and a huge pain in my ass.

I'd fucked a lot of women in this wonderful city, but I'd never fucked anyone the way I fucked Tatum Titan.

I was pretty sure she hadn't either.

She blew me off so easily, removed me from her life like a sweater she didn't want anymore. I didn't want to date this woman or become attached to her, but I didn't want to stop the greatest sex I'd ever had.

I was the greatest sex she'd ever had too.

It was a hunch.

But she blew me off anyway.

I tried to think of my next move, but I wasn't sure

how to proceed. Every attempt I made was blocked by her ruthlessness. The last time I succeeded, we were in a dark corner and my hard cock was pressed against that aching clit of hers. Making my move at her office, where there were glass doors that allowed the entire world to see what we were doing, probably wasn't the best idea.

Since she was so secretive about her sex life.

She wouldn't even tell me if she was fucking Thorn Cutler.

Fucking asshole.

Pine walked right through my office doors, bypassing my assistants because he thought he had the right to come and go whenever he pleased. "You don't have plans for Saturday, right?"

"Depends." I rubbed my fingertips against my jaw, feeling the scruff because I skipped the shave that morning.

"Now you do. We're taking your yacht for a ride."

"My yacht?" I cocked an eyebrow, always surprised my best friend demanded whatever he wanted. "Do I look like Santa Claus to you?"

"I'm not asking you to give it to me. And you're invited."

"Lucky me."

"I met this girl the other night, and she's coming along."

"I don't do threesomes."

Pine fell into the chair facing my desk, taking up as much space as possible since he made himself at home. "Yes, you do."

"Not with dudes."

"Anyway, she's bringing some friends along. Tell me you're down."

Ordinarily, I would jump at the opportunity to spend the day boating in the Atlantic with beautiful women on board. But right now, my eyes were set on one gorgeous brunette who had an ass that wouldn't quit. "Not interested."

"You've got to be kidding me. What's your deal?"

"I just don't want to go."

"Because you're still obsessed with Tatum Titan?" he asked incredulously. "She doesn't want to suck your dick. Get over it."

On the contrary, I was sure she did. "It's not about her."

"Yes, it is. I've been your friend for how many years now? I know when you want to fuck a lady. But in this case, you aren't gonna get your way."

Keeping my secret was a lot harder than I thought it would be.

"You're coming."

Pine was a like child sometimes. He didn't stop until he got his way. "Fine."

"Great." As soon as the details had been squared away, he changed the subject to the next thing we liked to talk about—besides women. "Rumor has it Bruce Carol is going under."

"Really?" Now he had my full focus. "Where did you hear this?"

"Roger. But I looked into it, and his stocks are dipping."

I'd have to delve into this more.

"He made a lot of rookie mistakes that never should have happened. But now someone is going to be even richer than they were before."

I rested my arms on my dark desk, looking right at my friend but thinking about something else entirely. "Yeah. Me."

———

THE YACHT WAS SITTING in the harbor, packed with cold liquor, sandwiches, and sunscreen.

"When are they gonna be here?" Mike asked, standing in his black swim trunks without his shirt.

"Any minute now," Pine said. "You know how women are. Just remember how hot they are."

Mike drank his beer, silenced by that comment.

Maybe if I fucked this woman, I would forget about the woman who had the audacity to blow me off. I hadn't realized how much I liked the chase until a woman actually made me work for it. She was the first one who didn't give me what I wanted right on the spot. She made me feel unremarkable.

And that only made me want to prove her wrong.

A black Cadillac pulled up to the edge of the harbor, sleek and shiny. The back door opened, and a long leg emerged, fitting into a nude wedge.

"That's them," Pine said. "I got the bottom loft."

"Top," Mike called.

That left me with the master, even though I wasn't sure if I would use it or not.

The women all got out of the car with their purses over their shoulders. In summer dresses with their bikinis underneath, they looked exactly like the kind of women we liked to party with.

But when they came closer, I recognized the one on the far left.

Tatum Titan.

I didn't grin too often, but now I couldn't suppress

my smile. My entire body tightened as she approached, arousal and excitement dissolving into my blood. She wore aviator sunglasses that hid her eyes from view. If she recognized me, she brushed it off and didn't break her stride. She failed to show any expression besides confidence. Surprise and fear weren't in her vocabulary.

Pine helped his date into the boat. "Hey, sweetheart."

"Hey." She kissed him on the cheek before they walked away to the other side of the boat.

Mike extended his hand and helped the blonde up. Judging by his smile, he was genuinely happy to see his date for the afternoon.

I didn't bother extending my hand to Titan, knowing she wouldn't take it. She made it up the steps with ease, her heels not slowing her down even though there wasn't much friction between the bottom of her shoe and the smooth surface of the yacht. When she reached the top, she faced me, her curled hair blowing in the slight breeze. "Hunt."

I still wore my grin. "Titan."

She glanced at her two friends, who were already being pampered with glasses of wine and male affection. She turned back to me, keeping her sunglasses on. Red lipstick was on her mouth, and a creamy tint was noticeable on her shoulders where she had applied sunscreen.

"What a nice surprise."

She turned her gaze and looked out onto the open waters of the Atlantic. Strands of hair came loose in the breeze, crossing over her face and sticking to her lipstick for just an instant. "It's a beautiful day. Let's enjoy it."

———

I ANCHORED the yacht a few miles off the coast, providing us a great view of the skyscrapers of the city. There were no other boats around, just us in the endless blue. I was the conductor of this voyage because I wasn't going to let any of the guys touch my yacht.

She was all mine.

We sat together in the back of the boat, comfortable on the soft cushions by a table laden with the snacks my crew prepared. Pine had his arm around Isa, so absorbed in her that he didn't seem to notice anyone else was there. Mike fed Pilar a grape, dropping the fruit into her mouth.

They would definitely be fucking.

Titan and I sat beside each other, drinking wine.

Pine opened a bottle and poured glasses all around. When she didn't object and drank it just as quickly as I did, I learned she liked other liquor besides whiskey.

"The famous Tatum Titan," Pine said as he looked at her. "I'm glad you're here. Hunt can't stop talking about you."

Titan didn't react, only sipping her wine.

I couldn't shoot him a glare since I wore my sunglasses. Last thing I needed was Titan to think I was talking about the way she rode my cock. When I told her I would protect her reputation, I meant it.

"He can't?" Titan asked. "Why is Hunt so interested in me?" With her legs crossed and her gorgeous body hidden underneath her dress, she looked more like a supermodel than her friend Pilar.

"Well, on paper, he's interested in your publishing business," Pine said. "But in reality, he just wants to—"

"Pine." All I needed to say was his name to get him to shut up.

Pine shut his mouth, but his eyes still sparkled with mischief. "He thinks you're pretty. I'll leave it at that."

After more conversation, the guys broke apart with their dates. Pine went to the loft downstairs, and Mike took Pilar in the other bedroom on the yacht.

Titan and I were finally alone together, but we weren't having fun like everyone else.

I left the seat and walked to the rail, seeing the city in all its glory. It was fabulous up close from my office window, but it was a different sight from a vantage point like this. Somehow, it made the gargantuan city seem small.

Titan came to my side, her hands resting on the edge. "Beautiful, huh?"

"There are no words."

She ran her fingers through her soft hair, looking sexy without even trying. She constantly put up a front of strength, something that was intentional. But when she looked desirable, that was all natural.

She didn't even need to try.

I pivoted my body so I faced her, our bodies close enough that I could touch her if I repositioned myself. "I didn't tell them."

At this angle, I could see her eyes behind her sunglasses. They were focused on the city miles away. "I know. But you obviously like to talk about me." The corners of her mouth rose in a smile.

"I do."

"And what kind of things do you say?"

"I'm frustrated I'm not getting what I want."

She still wore her slight smile. "Because I refuse to sell my company?"

I nodded. "But they think I just want to fuck you."

"Are they wrong?" she asked quietly.

"Right on the money, actually." I moved into her until my body was pressed against her shoulder. My fingers found the strap to her summer dress, recognizing the designer label sticking out from the back, and I slowly pulled it down until her bare shoulder was completely revealed.

She didn't stop me, remaining still as a statue. But her breathing gave her away, its escalation telling me she was tingling with excitement. My touch scorched her, burned her with my desire.

I pressed my lips to her skin, giving her a kiss so innocent it was dirty. It was a mere hint of what I wanted to do with her right now. I wanted to plow my cock inside her for the entire afternoon, making the boat rock from my thrusts. I gave her some of my tongue then sucked the skin, my teeth grazing her.

An imperceptible moan escaped her lips. It was so quiet, I wasn't sure I heard it before it was carried away on the sea breeze.

My mouth trailed up her neck until it rested

against her ear. I kissed the shell, the soft skin that was usually hidden underneath her hair.

She tensed underneath me, her body reacting just the way it did when our naked limbs were tangled together.

"Were you surprised to see me?"

"Yes."

"Looks like the universe wants us to be together."

She turned her head toward me but didn't pull her body away. "I think the universe is threatened when two suns exist in the same galaxy."

I kissed her hairline, my hands starting to explore her body. "What would happen if two suns combined together?" I slowly turned her body until she was facing me and the railing of the deck was behind her. I got her exactly where I wanted her, cornered, with my huge body hemming her in. She was like a wild animal that needed every protection in the world to keep her caged.

Her hands went to my stomach, the bottom of my six-pack. Her fingers felt the grooves in detail, feeling the mountains of muscle and the valleys of softness. They slowly slid up until her fingertips reached my muscular chest. Like our last conversation never happened, she touched my body as if it was under her ownership.

My hands gripped her dress and hiked it above her waist, leaving her bikini bottoms exposed. She was still pressed against the railing, and she didn't try to run. She stayed put, letting my massive body pin her in the perfect spot.

I pulled her sunglasses off her face and hooked them on the front of her dress, wanting to look her in the eye. Now that she didn't have a shield to hide behind, her words were obvious like a document on a computer screen. I could see her desire, see her need to be fucked by me.

My hand slid up the back of her neck, underneath the fall of her hair, and my palm cupped the back of her head. My lips were dangerously close to hers, close enough that I could take her mouth the instant I decided to. "You know what happens when they combine together?" I whispered. "They explode." My mouth moved to hers, and I kissed her softly, taking my sweet time because nothing was going to interrupt us. We'd been more focused on screwing, but never kissing. And kissing sounded like the sexiest thing in the world in that moment.

Her lips hesitated at the initial contact, quivering the second she felt the restrained intensity of my mouth. Her fingers dug into my chest slightly, her nails teasing me with their sharpness. As if she'd never kissed me before, she breathed in deeply before she kissed me back, her arousal burning throughout her body.

My thumb brushed against her cheek as I kissed her, our lips coming together, breaking apart, and then coming together again. Sometimes I ended the kiss just to rub my nose against hers, to memorize the sexy expression on her face. When I pressed my mouth to hers once more, she met me with a hungry embrace.

We moved together, our mouths turning to get as much of the other person as possible. When she gave me her small tongue, I greeted it with my own. We exchanged breaths as well as kisses, our embrace growing more heated. My hand gripped her hips where I held her dress up, and my cock nearly broke through my trunks in an attempt to get free.

I could lead her to my quarters so we could screw in private, just like my other two friends. But her reputation had to remain untouched, and I would never tarnish it unless she specifically asked me to.

But I had to do something.

I grabbed the back of her knee and swung her leg around my waist, having her ankle hook on to my hip. My hand gripped the back of her thigh and held her in place as I kept the kiss going, feeling her nipples all the way through her bikini top and dress. I pressed into her, getting my cock right against that nub I'd become acquainted with.

She moaned into my mouth, her arms now around my neck.

I gently ground against her, rubbing my rock-hard cock against her aching folds.

Her body reciprocated, taking my cock and moving with me at the same time. Her kisses became hungrier, taking my mouth with the kind of aggression she'd never shown before. She sucked my bottom lip into her mouth, eating me alive.

God, this woman.

Her hand gripped my ass, and she pulled me into her harder, pressing my cock perfectly against her clitoris. She ground against me, dry-humping me right on the deck of my yacht.

Feeling her want me so viciously, taking exactly what she wanted without waiting for me to offer it, was hot as fuck. I breathed into her mouth and gripped her hair, feeling my body yearn for a woman like I'd never had before. Every part of me ached for her. My cock wanted to claim every opening she had, to stuff her with come until she was overflowing. I'd always been a sexual man, but she turned me into a beast.

Her lips suddenly became immobile, unable to kiss me at all. Her nails dug into me, and her breaths became strained. Deeper and deeper they went, hoarse and quiet.

I rocked into her harder, staring at her face as I prepared for the show. She was shaking underneath my touch, her body prepared to fire off an orgasm that would make her moan louder than she wanted.

She gripped my biceps for balance and then came, panting against my mouth with a quiet moan accompanying it. My cock hardened at her pleasure, pressing against her harder. Her climax stretched on as long as it did when I was buried inside her. Her cheeks flushed bright red, and her eyes closed as she restrained herself from screaming in orgasmic relief. My mouth against hers seemed to be the only thing keeping her quiet.

She rocked her hips against me until the climax passed. She slowly drifted back down to reality, the ache between her legs gone now that she was satisfied. She pressed her forehead against mine as she caught her breath. Once it was over and we could hear the sound of the waves licking the sides of the yacht, we were back to the real world.

Her hands remained on my arms, and she looked down, avoiding my gaze.

It was the first time I'd seen her do that. "Titan."

"Yes?"

"Tell me what you want, and I'll give it to you."

She kept her face down, her hands resting on my arms.

"Titan."

"You can't."

"Try me." What did this woman want that I couldn't possibly give? She wanted a strong man to fuck her, and that's exactly what I could offer her. There was no stipulation that I would mind. If she had weird kinks, I was okay with that too.

"Trust me, you can't."

"No, trust me," I pressed. "I can."

NINE

Tatum

THE GIRLS LEFT WITH THE GUYS, GOING BACK TO their apartments even though they'd spent the entire afternoon screwing on the yacht.

I was jealous.

Hunt handed the keys over to his crew, and they took care of docking the ship and putting it back in the slip. We didn't clean up the mess we made, so I assumed that was being handled too.

We were alone again, and I knew exactly what conversation we were going to have.

Hunt came to my side, and like he had every right in the world, he grabbed my hand. His muscular hand overwhelmed mine, and he led me to the car he left in the parking lot. He stared me down like he dared me to object.

After my little performance on the boat, I didn't have the confidence to do anything.

He opened the passenger door to his red Lamborghini and got in the driver's seat. He didn't ask me if I wanted to be taken home before he started to drive, heading to his penthouse, I was certain.

We didn't speak on the drive.

I was still in my soaked bottoms and dress. My hair was a mess from the wind, and my nose was a little red despite all the sunscreen I'd put on. It was nighttime now, so my sunglasses were stowed away in my bag.

Hunt pulled into the parking garage of his building then killed the engine.

"Your car is beautiful." I broke the tension with a simple compliment, knowing the best way into a man's brain was through his toys.

"Thank you." He got out and took me by the hand again.

I felt like a couple going home after a long double date.

I didn't like that feeling.

We rode the elevator directly into his penthouse, the doors opening to a perfectly designed living space with classical music playing in the background. It must come on automatically as soon the doors opened.

"Something to drink?"

"Water, please."

He grabbed two glasses from the kitchen and handed me one.

I took a long drink, dehydrated from all the wine, whiskey, and hormones I'd indulged in all day.

He drank his water as he watched me, his masculine throat shifting as he consumed the entire glass effortlessly. He set the glass on the coffee table.

I did the same.

I assumed he wanted to get off since he did all the pleasing that afternoon. Getting rid of his blue balls sounded appetizing to me, not selfish on his part at all. He was one of the few men I would gladly get on my knees for and suck his enormous cock—even if it made me gag.

Instead of taking me into the bedroom, he continued to stand there in front of me, his eyes two smoking guns. He suffocated me naturally with his firmness, the authority he always exerted over me anytime we were in the same room together.

I felt like I was looking at a different version of myself. "Did you bring me here to stare?"

"Among other things." He stepped closer to me,

his gaze cold and warm at the same time. "We'll get to the good stuff in a second. But first, we're going to continue our conversation."

"What conversation?"

"The only conversation we've been having since we met."

I brushed it off, wanting to avoid the truth as much as possible. "I'm not selling my company."

"We'll get to that at another time."

"Really?" I cocked my head to the side, challenging his assurance.

He stood in front of me, the smell of cologne and sunscreen wafting into my nose. "Let's agree on one thing. We're gonna keep crossing paths, and every time we do, we're gonna end up in bed together."

Despite my previous mistakes, I wouldn't allow that to continue. I'd already crossed too many lines as it was.

"Every time I pursue you, we're just making it more obvious to the people around us that we're screwing. I don't want that, and neither do you. So let's come up with an arrangement."

"There's no arrangement that could work for us."

"I disagree."

He would always disagree until he got his way. I crossed my arms over my chest, blocking him with an invisible rope. "Tonight is the last night this is going to happen. I say we enjoy it before we forget about it."

He cocked his head to the side, downplaying my words without making a single argument. "How many times have you said that now?"

Asshole. "I only let you have me again because I thought that would be enough for you to forget about me."

"Forget about you?" he questioned. "Actually, you have the opposite effect on me. Now that I've had some of you, I want all of you. I haven't even fucked that pretty little mouth of yours yet. And don't get me started on that ass."

The blood drained from my face because it was headed in one direction—south. No man had ever spoken to me that way—and pulled it off.

"You're hiding something from me."

A lot of things, actually.

"You want me. I know you do. I made you come by dry-humping you. So let's not pretend otherwise."

I wasn't.

"And I want you too. There's no reason why we can't keep doing this—until one of us gets bored."

The more he pursued me, the more I wanted to be honest about my intentions. The more I wanted to come clean about the monster I was. But I would put my entire career on a platter in front of him—and a butcher knife in his hand. "Hunt, there's a lot more to me than meets the eye. I enjoy things that you don't understand. I have a life that resembles the underworld. There are things about me that I could never share. You want us to keep doing this, but honestly, I don't. If we stayed together, I'd want to make a lot of changes. And trust me when I say you wouldn't be into them."

His eyes were glued to my face. "How will you know unless you try?"

"Because I don't trust you, Hunt."

"You should."

"Why? You're my competitor and a stranger."

"But I'm also a man, the kind of man who would respect the wishes of his partner no matter what. Above all else, I believe in honesty and loyalty. If you ask for my loyalty, all I ask is you give me yours too."

My eyes shifted back and forth between his, sizing him up.

"Titan." The bite of his tone faded when he said my name. "Tell me exactly what you want. If you're right and it's something I'm not willing to do, then we'll forget the whole thing. But you shouldn't throw this away because you think you know me. You say

I'm a stranger. If that's the case, then you have no idea what my opinions are. I won't make assumptions about you if you do the same for me."

Somehow, he softened my hard edges, making me smooth underneath. I didn't see him as a threat anymore, even somewhat of a friend. He did it so easily, said it with such pretty words. I felt like I could trust a man I didn't know.

How did he do that?

"Titan." He stepped forward, completely invading my personal space. His face was just inches from mine, the smell of his body soap still noticeable under the sunscreen. "Trust me."

Trust was the most prized word in my dictionary. I was lucky enough to have a few people whom I trusted with my darkest secrets, but that kind of comfort didn't come easily. It took years, decades, to earn that kind of loyalty.

But he was already asking for it.

There was nothing I adored more than being with someone I trusted completely, to have the kind of relationship that was beautiful because it was unknown to the rest of the world. It allowed me to be me—in all my true colors. But loyal men were hard to find. "I'll think about it."

Hunt held his breath as he looked at me, approval

in his dark gaze. That was the most cooperation he would get out of me, and there was no point in pushing it. I'd given him something I hadn't given to anyone else. Every person I'd been with had been thoroughly investigated before I'd bothered.

But I was going into this blind.

TEN

Hunt

I FINALLY GOT A DIFFERENT ANSWER OUT OF HER besides no.

Maybe.

It wasn't a yes, but it would be soon.

I just had to be patient.

I didn't know what skeletons she was hiding in her closet. I didn't know what kind of kinky shit she enjoyed. And whatever sinful stuff she was into, I was surprised she was embarrassed about it.

She didn't seem like the kind of woman who embarrassed easily.

I wondered if she was into whips and chains, being tied up while I fucked her with a mask on. If that was her thing, that was fine by me. The kinkier, the better. I'd whip her ass as many times as she asked.

I'd dominate her like she'd never been dominated before.

Piece of cake.

But if it were that simple, she would have just told me.

Natalie spoke through the intercom. "Sir, I have Pine Rosenthal here to see you."

I made sure my assistants understood he couldn't just barge into my office anymore. Even if we had been friends since grade school, that didn't matter. He could wait like everyone else. "Send him in."

Pine walked inside, glowering at me like I stabbed him in the gut. "What the hell? Why do I have to wait?"

"You aren't special. That's why."

Pine fell into the chair and rolled his eyes like a child.

I did feel like the adult in most situations. "How's Isa?"

"Gorgeous and flexible." He winked. "I can't tell you how I know that."

"I didn't ask."

"So…did you fuck Titan yet?"

I was fucking her, but the question annoyed me. The basic question almost seemed disrespectful toward her. Pine was my friend, but he obviously saw her as something that should be conquered, as if bedding a strong woman like her was some kind of special accomplishment.

Now I understood why she didn't want me to say anything. All the guys in our universe would talk about it. She would be seen as the woman who opened her legs for me, and she would lose respect because of it.

Bullshit.

"No."

"Really?" Both of his eyebrows nearly popped off his face. "She won't give it up, will she?"

"She's not going to. We're just friends."

"Yeah, okay," he said sarcastically. "And my cock is just friends with Isa's pussy."

I threatened him with a single look.

Pine finally shut his mouth. "Is she seeing someone, then?"

"No. I think she's just picky about who she dates."

"And Diesel Hunt didn't make the cut?"

"Guess not."

"She's probably damaged goods anyway since her boyfriend died…"

My spine went rigid when that piece of information was laid out on the table. When I researched her, I found information about her professional career, how she started with nothing, and made it to the top on her own. There was nothing written about her personal life, not even a single boyfriend. "When did this happen?"

"A long time ago, in her early twenties. She wasn't well-known at the time."

"I didn't see anything like that online."

"That doesn't surprise me. I'm sure she went to great lengths to prevent that information from circling. Most people don't know about it because it happened so long ago when she was a nobody."

"How do you know about it?"

"My dad told me."

I wanted to know every little detail about this, but I didn't want to sound too eager. "What happened to him?"

"They were living together, and there was some kind of break-in. She was beat up pretty badly, had to stay in the hospital for a while. The guy was killed by the robber, stabbed right in the heart. Brutal, man. Happened in Brooklyn."

I stared at my friend with a blank look on my face, but there were a million thoughts circling in my mind. She lived through such a brutal attack, but the man she loved didn't survive. He probably died trying to protect her.

No wonder why she was so closed off now. "Do you remember exactly when this happened?"

"I think she was twenty-one."

That was nine years ago. She still hadn't moved on? That night haunted her dreams? "Thanks for letting me know…"

"So maybe it's better that things didn't work out."

"Yeah…"

ELEVEN

Tatum

———

A week passed.

I got a lot of work done, but every time someone walked into my office, I glanced up to see who it was.

To see if it was him.

Hunt gave me more space than he had before, knowing I was considering telling him everything I was hiding.

I went back and forth a lot.

Sometimes, I thought it would be fine and I should just tell him the truth. And other times, I realized it was a terrible idea with deadly repercussions.

So I decided to ask someone I trusted more than anyone else in the world.

Thorn.

He walked into my apartment and joined me in the kitchen. "Smells good."

"Sirloin with asparagus."

"I'm glad you invited me over."

We sat together in my dining room, next to the floor-to-ceiling windows that overlooked the entire city. The bright lights twinkled across the skyline, the lit-up bridge in the distance. Car lights could be seen everywhere, growing bright when they faced us head on, and then disappearing when they turned a different way.

Thorn ate quietly, a glass of red wine beside his plate. He was dressed down in a pair of denim jeans and a black t-shirt, the fabric hugging the prominent muscles of his body. He worked out religiously to maintain his body. I, on the other hand, just didn't eat. I had everything I could possibly want, but I still couldn't afford the luxury of time.

Thorn switched his gaze to me. "What did you want to talk to me about?"

"What makes you think I want to talk about anything?" I cut into my asparagus before I placed it in my mouth.

"Sweetheart, I know you." He took a bite of his steak then immediately drank his wine afterward. "What is it?"

I held my glass wine before I answered. "Diesel Hunt."

"What about him?"

"He's been adamant about having something long-term with me." The sex wouldn't be like it was now, but that was because it would be better. He might disagree, but that was his own decision to make.

"And?"

"I'm thinking of telling him my preferences." I drank my wine to mask the unease I felt in my stomach. Fear wasn't something that grasped me often, but when it did, it felt like a rock in the pit of my stomach.

"Diesel Hunt doesn't seem like the kind of guy you're looking for."

"I know." But I wanted him anyway. I would love to strip everything away and just be who I was.

"Can he keep his mouth shut?"

"He says loyalty is important to him."

Thorn continued eating, considering what I said. "Sounds like you made up your mind."

"Just wanted your opinion about it."

"As long as you keep my secret, I don't care."

"You know I always will."

"But if this develops into something more—"

"It won't."

Thorn didn't press me on it, knowing I always stuck to my guns. "What will you say if he asks about us?"

"Nothing. It's none of his business."

"He might want more of an explanation."

"I'll come up with something if I have to."

He chewed a piece of asparagus before he nodded. "Make him sign an NDA."

I did it with all my partners. No reason why I shouldn't do it with Hunt. "I will."

"Good luck," he said. "I hope it works out for you, but I suspect it won't."

I expected Hunt to walk away once my offer was on the table. But even with low expectations, I knew how disappointed I would be if that were our last interaction. No one could make my thighs clench the way he did.

And no one probably ever would.

———

GETTING his phone number wasn't difficult. All I had to do was pull a few strings, and within two minutes, it was programmed into my phone. Instead of texting him, I called him. This wasn't any different from a business meeting and deserved a far more personal touch.

He answered the phone, his voice deep and heavy with masculinity. I could picture the movement of his lips when he spoke, the way his throat shifted when he smiled. "Hunt."

"Titan."

A long pause ensued, full of that smile I knew was plastered across his face. "Lovely to hear from you."

I was sitting at my desk with my legs crossed, his male voice making my body do particularly female things. Butterflies didn't swirl in my stomach, but my breathing escalated when I pictured his mouth against mine. "Let's schedule a meeting. Let me know when you're free."

"For you, I'm free anytime."

Now a grin formed on my face. "Tonight. 7 p.m. My place."

"I finally get to see your place. I'll be there."

"Goodbye, Hunt."

"Titan, whatever agreement we reach, I'm fucking you before I leave."

Heat moved up my throat, like flames that grew in the fireplace when another log was tossed on top. My slender legs were pressed tightly together, and I automatically licked my lips in response. "I'd expect nothing less."

———

MY PENTHOUSE WAS JUST like my office, in shades of black, gray, and white. Pops of color from flowers, decorative pillows, and blankets brought warmth and light into the room. A soft rug was on the ground, and my favorite paintings were on the walls.

The lights were down low, everything was set up at the dining table, and I was already helping myself to my favorite drink before the elevator beeped with his arrival.

The doors opened, and there he stood, six foot three of all man. He wasn't in his suit, having changed before he came over. Now he was wearing jeans and an olive-green t-shirt, his muscular arms visible, acting as eye candy.

And arm porn.

He stepped inside like he owned the place—and me. His eyes were on me, not taking in the features of the entryway or living room. He didn't seem to care about anything inside except me.

I stayed in my seat at the head of the table, refusing to stand and address him. Giving him a handshake felt inappropriate, and a kiss on the cheek would lead to kisses in other places. "Can I get you something to drink?"

He grabbed my drink before he took a seat at the opposite end of the table. With his eyes on me, he drained the glass into his mouth before he set it down. "I'm good." I'd done the same thing to him in my office, and it wasn't lost on me why he was doing it now.

I pulled out the NDA and a pen and slid it toward him. "I need you to sign this."

He kept his gaze on me for several long seconds before he looked down. He barely glanced at it before he looked up again. "A nondisclosure agreement?" That handsome eyebrow was hiked up, incredulity accenting his sexy look.

"Yes."

He eyed it again before he turned it over. "I'm not signing it."

My hands were together on the table, and I cocked my head even though I tried not to let my temper rise. "Then we have nothing to discuss. You can show yourself out, Hunt."

He didn't move a fraction of an inch. "I don't need to sign it because it's a moot point. We're both equally wealthy. We can sue each other back and forth until the end of time, accomplishing nothing in the process. This sort of thing doesn't work between two parties such as ourselves."

He was absolutely right, but I refused to admit it. "Then you should have no problem signing it."

"This relationship you want to have is going to be based on trust—that goes both ways. That needs to start now. Having me sign this takes away that level of trust."

"How can I trust you unless you give me a reason to?"

"My friends question me about you every single day. I've never told them about the things we do when we're alone together, no matter how dirty they are. I've kept that to myself, and I will continue to do so until you say otherwise. I've already proven myself to you."

He had done as I asked, and I couldn't argue otherwise.

Hunt watched me closely. "Now talk to me, Titan. Whatever we discuss in here dies with us."

Something about Hunt drew me in, led me to believe I could trust him even though I didn't have a concrete reason why I could. He reminded me of Thorn in a lot of ways. Perhaps that was another reason why I liked him. He was honest to a fault and transparent. There was never a time when I couldn't figure out what he was thinking. And if I couldn't, all I had to do was ask. "Very well."

Hunt sat forward in his chair, his hands on the table as he leaned toward me. He watched me with eyes that were the same color as the soil, the same color as the ground I walked on every single day. It reminded me of the rest of him, solid and thick.

"I have specific relationships with the men in my life. I wouldn't even call them relationships, just arrangements."

Hunt stared me down, hardly blinking.

"In these arrangements, I'm in absolute control. We do what I say, when I say it. There's no room for negotiation. The man is only responsible for following the orders that I give. His purpose is to please me, to fulfill the fantasies that I enjoy. The arrangement continues until one of us terminates it. There's no love or friendship. Just lust and trust."

Hunt still didn't change his expression, listening to everything I said with perfect attention. He didn't wear a mocking look or narrow his eyes in repulsion. He took it in all in—silently. "You're a Dominant."

At least he had a basis to understand what I was. "Close, but not quite."

"What's the difference?"

"In my world, there are no safe words. By signing yourself over to me, you're giving me your soul." It would be wrapped around my fingers for the entire duration. He would have no voice, no opinion. "Your only option is to leave. But once you do, you can't come back. Trust is broken, and the arrangement is over."

Hunt still didn't seem put off by any of this.

"It's more extreme, more disturbing."

Hunt rubbed his fingers over his chin, feeling the shadow that had formed across his face. His brown eyes didn't change in reaction, just as dark as they were before. "If we were in this arrangement right now, right this second, what would you do to me?"

I didn't need to work my imagination too hard. I held his expression, my gaze hard as steel. "Remove my panties and secure them around your wrists behind that chair."

Hunt's expression hardened.

"After that, I would get on my knees, suck you off, and then ride you, coming as many times as I wanted. Only when I was completely satisfied would I give you permission to come. And if you came sooner, I'd punish you."

His face flushed with heat, his throat shifting as he

swallowed. A slight grin stretched across his face. "Sounds pretty hot."

"Hotter than you can imagine."

Not all men took this in stride as well as he did. The dominant, authoritative men such as him weren't interested in being the plaything of a demanding woman like me. Hunt was the most confident man I'd ever known, his presence suffocating anytime he was nearby. But so far, he'd taken it the best.

That was something I didn't expect.

"I'd be your sex slave, pretty much," he said. "I'd fuck you when and where you'd like."

"Something like that."

He leaned back in the chair, his broad shoulders powerful no matter how he held himself. "I gotta say, I'm not seeing the downside to this. You're more than welcome to ride my dick as much as you want. And punish me all you like." He winked.

He only saw the good side to the arrangement, not the bad. "Can you handle taking orders from a woman?"

"When they're sexual in nature, why not? Boss me around all you like." He continued to wear a charming smile that melted all the panties in a one-mile radius.

"And what about when I want to hurt you?"

"You couldn't hurt me." His teasing nature disappeared, replaced by a shadow in his eyes. "Do your worst."

He didn't have a clue. "I have a room full of whips. Trust me, I could hurt you."

"Doubtful."

My eyes narrowed, surprised he was still sitting there. "Another part of the arrangement is my complete control. You don't talk unless I tell you to. When I tell you to be somewhere, you're there. When I tell you to touch me, not touch me, whatever, you obey. When I tell you to hook yourself to the ceiling, you do it. You're honestly telling me that's something you, Diesel Hunt, can do? It won't be the playful banter we have now. It'll all be business, no play."

He crossed his arms over his chest, relaxed in his chair like we were talking about dinner plans.

"It's not as easy as you think it is. I've had plenty of men walk away."

"You do this a lot?"

"For nearly ten years."

He cocked his head to the side slightly, absorbing everything like a dry sponge. "And you enjoy it?"

"Why else would I keep doing it this long?"

"You've never fallen in love?"

Only once—and that was a mistake. "Not in these arrangements, no. I'm not interested in love."

Hunt stared me down, his expression closed off and unreadable. "I need a rundown of exactly what I can expect before I give you my final answer."

"That's fair." I named off all the things he should be expected to do, explaining every precise detail.

"So, it's nothing but rough sex," he said. "Through and through."

"Through and through."

"There's no personal conversations, no sharing. You don't ask me anything personal, I don't ask you anything personal. Just like when you're at work, you do your hours then go home."

"Interesting."

"And this is a monogamous relationship. No one else but the two of us."

That arrogant smile came back. "You don't want to share me with anyone. That's cute."

"It's not about jealousy. It's about sexual health. I don't use condoms in these situations, and we both need to remain exclusive to this arrangement."

He nodded in understanding. "Sounds fair."

"So, what do you say?" I wanted him to say yes. In fact, I wanted him to say yes more than anyone else I'd ever been with. That body, that kiss, everything about him was magnetic. Being able to do whatever I wanted to him at any time sounded like the most appetizing thing in the world.

"I'll need to think about it." He broke eye contact and looked out at the city.

So he had doubts. "What is your hesitation? Perhaps that's something I can clarify."

He didn't turn his head back toward me, but his eyes shifted. His handsome smile was back again. "You want me to say yes."

"Obviously."

"But you really want me to say yes."

I shut my mouth, displaying my poker face once again.

He chuckled to himself. "You can whip me all you want. You can slap me until my face is red. You can do whatever you want to me, and I won't think twice about a safe word. But you're right about one thing. Having to obey you at all times would be a challenge. I'm used to being in charge. I'm used to issuing orders, not taking them. I think it'd be sexy in this situation, having a gorgeous woman tell me exactly how to fuck her. Having her tie me up so she can fuck me all she wants is nothing short of a fantasy. But after a while…I'd want to be the one to tie you up, to fuck you exactly as I please, to tell you exactly what to do, and get off to you obeying me."

"But that's not how it works. I'm in charge—you are not."

"That's exactly why I need to think about it." His eyes shifted out the window again, growing quiet like I wasn't there at all.

I watched him until my eyes shifted down to the paper in front of me. It had a few notes he'd made, points of negotiation for things he was unwilling to do. But he was open to every single request I made. All he needed to do was decide how much he was willing to give me, how much he was willing to sacrifice his own natural urges to fulfill mine. "You're right. I hope you do say yes."

He rapped his knuckles against the table before he stood up, sexy in his fitted t-shirt. "There's something I need to do before I go. And you know exactly what that is." His gaze bore into mine, hot and fiery. He slowly approached my end of the table until he came up behind my chair. Both of his hands rested on the back of my chair as he leaned over me. "Get your ass up. Now."

TWELVE

Hunt

THE OFFER WAS ON THE TABLE, BUT I WASN'T SURE if I was going to take it.

It was tempting.

But it was also unappetizing.

Having a gorgeous woman like her dominate me sounded like a real treat. Fucking her until she screamed, giving it to her exactly as she asked, sounded like something I would jerk off to anyway.

But I wanted to be in charge too. I didn't want my partner to be the one always calling the shots, taking away the power I desperately needed at times. It had to be equal, and she definitely didn't want equal.

But if I said no, I would lose her altogether.

That was an option I didn't want to take either. It was the first time I didn't crave a long line of women in my bed. Since the moment I met Titan, I hadn't even entertained the possibility of fucking someone else.

She was the only person I wanted to be with.

Something told me I should hold on to it, do something to claim this woman as mine. But since I'd never had such an experience before, I wasn't sure how to accomplish that. I'd never been with a woman for more than few weeks. And anything beyond a month was nonexistent. The constants in my life were my friends. They were my home base.

Never a woman.

Would Titan compromise with me?

Meet me halfway?

Who I was kidding? This was Tatum Titan, a woman who didn't compromise.

Why would I be any different?

In any other situation, I would discuss this with my friends. But since I promised Titan my loyalty, getting advice on the matter was impossible.

A week came and went, and I didn't contact her. I didn't stop by her office to say hi. I went to bed alone, using my hand to get myself off to memories of fucking her. Why couldn't we just be two people who fucked casually?

Why did she have to be into that?

It seemed like people who had twisted fetishes had

suffered painful lives. They were the victims of abuse, or they were just abandoned when they needed someone the most. Titan was such a strong figure it was hard to believe she had any problems.

But I didn't know her that well.

It'd only been a month since I met her, but I felt like I'd seen her smile enough times to know what made her laugh. I'd seen her wear the same brand of shoes enough times to know what her style was. I'd kissed her enough times to know she liked vanilla perfume and whiskey. I'd fucked her enough times to know exactly how to make her come.

But in reality, I really didn't know her at all.

———

WE SAT TOGETHER at the strip club, women dancing on poles in just their thongs. They swayed their hips to the music, their long hair stretching down their backs. The music played overhead, and everyone was enveloped in a sea of darkness.

A woman sat beside me on the couch, a pretty brunette whose name I couldn't remember. The guys had their own dates, neither one of them Titan's friends. Since I didn't want them to ask me any more questions about Titan, I didn't ask them any more questions about Pilar and Isa. But judging from the way they weren't thinking about them tonight, I didn't think the women were in the picture anymore.

"Do you like her, Diesel Hunt?" the brunette asked as she nodded to the dancing girl on the stage.

I'd been looking at her, but I was staring right through her. I didn't like it when people used my full name outside the office. Sounded strange coming from his woman, whose hand was sitting on my chest. "She's fine."

"I can dance for you…somewhere private."

The second a woman threw herself at me, my interest died away. Lately, it'd been hard for me to get excited about anything. I'd done everything fun in this city. I'd fucked everyone, drunk everything, and partied everywhere.

There wasn't anything else to do.

I'd hit a plateau—and I was only thirty-five. "Maybe some other time."

Pine noticed my forlorn expression and tapped me on the shoulder. "Dude, what's the deal? You've been a bummer all week."

I was a bummer because I knew what I had to do. "Not feeling well. I'll see you later." I pulled out of the woman's embrace, walked outside, and found my car parked along the street. The engine roared to life as soon as I started it, and the music came on through the luxurious sound system.

I pulled onto the road and drove through the streets of Manhattan, hitting traffic at times and having open streets at others. There wasn't a particular direction I was going. I had no agenda. I just didn't want to be in that club anymore—doing the same thing I'd done a hundred times.

I eventually found my way back to the parking garage of my building. I pulled in to my spot but didn't kill the engine. Instead, I searched through my phone until I found Titan's number. I stared at it for a long time before my finger finally hit the button.

She answered after a few rings, the sound of loud music coming through the speakers. She was out somewhere, hitting the town with her friends. I wondered if Thorn Cutler was with her, not that I should care. "Hey."

I listened to the music in the background and recognized the song. "Hey."

The music slowly faded away as she stepped outside or into the bathroom. "Everything alright?" Her voice surrounded me in the car, strong and beautiful to my ears.

"I've thought about your offer for the past week."

She turned quiet, giving me the space to say what I needed to say.

"As tempting as it sounded, I'm gonna have to turn it down."

Silence.

It was stupid to expect her to argue with me, to persuade me to change my mind. She put her offer on the table and wasn't going to change it. There was no compromise. Being with Titan was exciting because she wasn't like other women. She had a brain, and she knew how to use it. She was strong, unbreakable. I found a successful and daring woman like her to be the sexiest thing on the planet. "As I promised, this stays between you and me. Good luck, Titan."

She continued to remain quiet.

Was she going to say something to change my mind?

Titan finally spoke. "Thank you for letting me know. Take care, Hunt." As if this were nothing but a business call, she hung up.

I heard the line go dead in my car, her abrupt goodbye. The disappointment shouldn't fill me, but it did. It was heavy, like a bullet in my flesh. When she made the offer to me, I assumed that meant I was special to her.

But no one was special to her.

I finally turned off my car and walked into my penthouse—alone.

———

"HERE'S YOUR TUX." Natalie walked inside and hung up my dry cleaning on the coat rack. "Your shopper also picked up this watch for you." She set the box on the edge of the desk. "She thought it would go well with your outfit."

"Thank you, Natalie."

"Anything else, sir?"

"No, thank you."

Natalie walked out and left me alone.

My cell phone rang, and Pine's name appeared on the screen.

I answered it. "Hey."

"Going to the Met Gala tonight?"

"Yep." It was a time to give back to charity, but also to further my own business agenda. Always being aware of potential deals, rising and falling business opportunities, as well as your competitors, was key to staying on the Forbes List.

"Taking anyone?"

I never took anyone to these things—and he knew that. "No. You?"

"I'm flying solo tonight. Dad wants me to go."

"You can be his eyes and ears."

"So, you wanna pick me up?"

I chuckled into the phone. "You aren't bumming a ride off me, man."

"Damn, I had to try. Hey, I heard Titan is going to be there."

Another week had gone by, and I hadn't heard from her. It was safe to say she wouldn't put any other deal on the table. She wasn't bluffing when she said she didn't compromise. I fucked her before I left her penthouse, and I was still jerking off to the memory every night. I imagined how it would feel to be tied up so she could ride my cock all she wanted—bareback. It always got my engine going. "Why would I care about that?"

"Are you still trying to acquire her publishing house?"

I didn't care about it anymore. "Not sure. Now that Bruce Carol has hit hard times, that might be a better opportunity."

"True."

"I've got work to do, Pine. I'll talk to you later."

"And you don't think I'm working?"

My silence was the only answer he needed.

"Alright, I'm just fucking around. You caught me." He hung up.

——————

MY DRIVER OPENED the back door, and I stepped out to a sea of reporters. I buttoned the front of my suit as I walked forward, ignoring the flashes from all the camera. A few reporters tried to get my attention by calling my name, but I ignored them as I stepped inside the hotel.

A crystal chandelier hung from the ceiling, the meticulously cut shards reflecting the lights. Music played overhead, so soft I could hardly heard it. A few couples stood in the lobby in their expensive gowns and tailored suits, talking amongst themselves before entering the ballroom.

With one hand in my pocket, I walked toward the ballroom. Long golden pipes hung from the ceiling, and the walls were blanketed with lights that looked like stars. The tables had white tablecloths with large vases filled with white lilies. It was like every other charity event I'd been to, where the party itself was worth more than the money that was actually raised.

My eyes ached to search for Titan, wondering if

she would be staring at me when our eyes met. What gown was she wearing? Would she look more beautiful than I'd ever seen her? Would she think about the last night we were together? Or was I some forgotten memory she didn't think twice about?

I ran into a few colleagues and engaged in small talk before a waiter handed me a flute of champagne. Still bubbling and golden, it fizzled as the bubbles rose to the surface. I took a sip, knowing I'd tasted something much sweeter off Titan's lips.

My eyes landed across the room, and I spotted her. My mind immediately shifted that way, unconsciously detecting the magnetic energy she emitted. She owned every room she stepped into, just as she owned every person.

Except me.

Beside her was the infamous Thorn Cutler, a businessman known for his capitalistic approach to brand awareness. With a height similar to mine, he complemented her perfectly. He had handsome features that attracted the attention of most women. Possessing a square jaw, bright eyes, and massive shoulders, he had the whole package. And not to mention, he had money too.

His hand moved to the small of her back, guiding

her around a group of people who were talking over their champagne.

Rage.

Anger.

Blind jealousy.

I felt so many things I wasn't familiar with. I'd never been possessive over a woman. Pine and I shared women all the time. When a woman walked out of my apartment after a fun night, I didn't think about her twice.

But watching Titan with another man made me sick.

I didn't understand their relationship. Every time I asked, she deflected the conversation. Sometimes, they seemed like they were together, like right now, and at others, they seemed indifferent to each other. I took Titan out of a club and fucked her at my place. It didn't seem like Thorn even knew she was gone.

So what was the deal?

I turned my gaze away before she noticed I was staring at her. I might cross paths with her during the night, and I would give a polite hello. But I wouldn't go out of my way to speak to her—even if I was still dreaming about her.

"You made it." Pine appeared at my side and clapped me on the shoulder. "Nice party, right?"

I drank my champagne. "Not bad."

"The CEO of Maxwell is here." Pine nodded discreetly to a man in a dark suit. "I love his cars. Thinking about getting one."

"Would you like an introduction?"

Pine looked like a boy who just saw a mound of Christmas presents underneath his tree. "You know him?"

I'd partied with him a few times. "Yeah."

Pine's eyes were about to pop out of his head. "Hell yeah, I wanna meet him. Just make me look good, alright?"

I chuckled. "Alright."

———

TITAN AND THORN were together the entire time. They never held hands or shared a kiss, but his arm was usually around her waist. For not being a couple, they seemed to be a couple.

But she asked me to be hers.

Did that mean Thorn was hers in the meantime?

Was she fucking him while she was fucking me?

Since she was committed to monogamy, that didn't seem likely.

I walked up to the bar to get another drink, in the

mood for an Old Fashioned. Whenever Titan was near me, that was what I craved. I wouldn't mind pouring it all over her body and licking it up.

"Looks like we have the same taste in drinks." Thorn appeared at my side and ordered two Old Fashioneds from the bartender.

I pivoted my body toward him, hating him even more now that he was right beside me. He possessed a natural air of confidence, of magnetism. It rivaled my own, but I shouldn't expect anything less from Tatum Titan. She'd only be interested in men who could project the same sense of strength. "Looks like we have the same taste in a lot of things."

Catching on to exactly what I meant, he smiled. "I'll drink to that." He grabbed the glass off the counter and took a drink. "It's too bad the two of you couldn't reach a compromise. I think you would have enjoyed it."

I kept up my poker face, absorbing everything and revealing nothing in return. Thorn was fully aware of Titan's preferences, obviously. But again, he didn't seem to care. If they were together, they must have an open relationship of some sort. Or they weren't together at all. I really didn't know anything about Thorn Cutler. "I'm sure I would have—but only for so long."

"Then propose a compromise. Negotiate. You're good at doing that, Diesel Hunt."

I cocked my head slightly, unsure what game he was playing. "Titan doesn't make compromises."

"You're right, she doesn't." He stepped closer to me, lowering his voice so no one else could hear what we were saying. "But I think she'd make one for you." He pulled away and winked. "You didn't hear that from me." He took the two glasses and walked off. Titan was speaking to Jonathan Kyte, the founder Mach Six, one of the biggest programming companies in the world. Her back was turned to us, so she didn't see the exchange.

Thorn had given me a lot to think about.

We sat down for dinner, Pine on my right and a few other associates at my table. Brett Maxwell sat beside me, a great innovator of cars. I liked his work, his sleek design, and his powerful engines. The two of us had a lot in common—more in common than most people realized.

"How are things with you?" Brett asked. Pine was chatting to Mike about the stock market, talking about finances like average people spoke about the weather.

"No complaints." Actually, just one complaint. "What about you?"

He adjusted his cuff link, surveying the ballroom with subtle indifference. "I'm launching a new line of cars next week. You should stop by for a private tour."

"I'm not gonna say no to that."

"Good." With hazelnut-colored eyes and a slight shadow on his chin, he had the same dark features I possessed. He wasn't as ruthless as I was, having the charm of a salesman. He started building his fortune at a young age, selling old cars on a lot. But he made a name for himself over the years. Now he was on top of the world, driving fast cars for a living with babes in the passenger seat. "I hoped you wouldn't." He surveyed the crowd again, on the verge of boredom.

"Wanna hit the links on Saturday?"

"Sure. I haven't broken out the clubs in a while."

"Looks like I'm gonna kick your ass, then."

The corner of his mouth rose in a smile. "We'll meet on the racetrack afterward. Then I'll kick your ass."

I chuckled. "Looks like we have a deal." I extended my hand.

He shook it. "Any special woman in your life, Diesel?"

He was one of the only people in the world who called me by my first name. Titan popped into my mind, but I couldn't share that information. "Not at the moment. You?"

"No. Just a line of faceless women, unfortunately."

"Unfortunately?" I asked.

He leaned toward me, our conversation turning private. "Remember when we were kids and all we wanted to eat was candy? But when we finally got our way, we got sick of it. It didn't matter how good or fresh it was. Always tasted like shit. That's how I'm starting to feel...the same old shit every day."

I knew all too well. "I share your misfortune."

"I guess I want something different, something I've never had before."

I got one taste of Titan, and now that was all I craved. She wiped my palate clean, gave me a new start.

Brett took a drink of his wine. "I guess men in our positions are never happy with what we have, huh?"

"We always want more."

He clinked his glass against mine. "Or we always want something particular."

———

THE PROGRAM ENDED, celebrating how much

money we'd raised for the Red Cross. Everyone clapped before they continued to enjoy their evening, furthering their own ambitious agenda in the name of helping those less fortunate.

I wasn't judging. I was doing the exact same thing.

I headed to the bathroom, unaware of where Titan was. She was probably still sitting at her table with Thorn and the rest of the people who'd made it into her inner circle. I tried not to keep an eye on her, knowing that woman was aware of her surroundings at all times. I refused to show blatant interest.

I crossed the ballroom and entered the hallway. She happened to be coming the opposite direction, just finished using the restroom or making a phone call. Face-to-face and eye-to-eye, we looked at each other.

I stared her down and chose not to ignore her. I could have easily walked around her and pretended she didn't exist. But when those green eyes were on me, there was no possibility of looking away. She challenged me with a simple look, and I always met every challenge that came my way.

We stopped and stared at each other. She was in a deep blue gown with her hair pulled back into an elegant bun. I'd never seen her hair done that way before, showing more of her hypnotic face. She had sharp cheekbones, dazzling eyes, and a slender neck that had been marked with my kisses. I'd seen this woman naked several times, but she'd never looked more beautiful than she did in that moment. Diamond earrings were in her lobes, and they sparkled with such intensity that their brilliance couldn't be denied. Another diamond hung from her necklace, just as bright.

I refused to speak first. Whoever held their silence the longest always had the most power. I turned down her offer because I couldn't allow her to dominate me. Holding my tongue was another way of showing that.

She took the lead. "Hunt."

"Titan." We were alone in the hallway, but we spoke as though thousands of ears were listening in on our conversation. "Are you having a good time?"

"I suppose. You?"

I watched her lips move without really focusing on her words. "I suppose."

She held her black clutch in front of her, a designer handbag to add to the collection of others she already had in her beautiful penthouse. With her makeup done in this fashion, her eyes looked bigger and brighter than usual. I wondered how they would look if I made her come in the hallway, right up against the wall.

I slid my hands into the pockets of my suit, restraining myself from grabbing her the way I liked. "I see that Thorn Cutler is your date."

She held my gaze without blinking, but she refused to answer my question.

Just as stubborn as always.

"Did you bring anyone?"

"I never took you for a woman who played games." One of the things I liked about Titan was her honesty. She gave it to you straight, not considering your feelings on the matter. The fact that she was pretending not to know if there was a woman on my arm was beneath her.

Despite my insult, she didn't react. "I guess your answer is no, then."

"It's been no since I last saw you." I didn't need to tell her that information, and I wasn't sure why I did. I should let her imagination run wild, let her think a different woman was sleeping in my bed every night. If I was this jealous of Thorn Cutler, a man who obviously didn't care who Titan fucked, then she must be jealous too.

She tried to fight her reaction, but a tiny glimmer of softness shone through. She committed herself to being so hard all the time that she couldn't allow herself to express an instant of weakness—not ever. But she showed a little to me.

I stepped forward and placed the backs of my fingers against her cheek.

She inhaled a deep breath, her body reacting to my touch. She closed her eyes slightly, turning her cheek into the embrace like she wanted more.

My fingers trailed down to her neck, over her pulse in her neck. My eyes soaked in the appearance of her lips, the soft and luscious lips I'd kissed many times. I tilted my head closer to her, loving her height in those five-inch heels. It made it easier to kiss her, to lean in like this and press my mouth to hers.

Her lips were locked in place, feeling my mouth seal over hers. She didn't even breathe, her entire body shutting down in response.

My palm moved against her cheek, and I deepened the kiss, parting her lips with my own.

She came back to life instantly, overcoming the shock of my public kiss. She kissed me back, her lips gliding over mine as our warm flesh moved together. Her tongue was there for the taking, and I swiped mine against hers.

She moaned into my mouth, a breathless flutter that was too sexy for me to handle.

My hands moved to her waist, and I guided her against the wall, my kiss deepening and my arousal burning. My hand palmed the back of her head, and I ground into her, my cock pressed against her stomach through my tux pants. We shifted and moved together, and if she weren't wearing a long dress, her leg would be wrapped around my waist.

If we were alone, I'd be fucking her right now.

Her hands broke from their restraints, and she felt my body, gliding over my muscles through my tuxedo and feeling my strength. Her fingertips touched my chin, feeling the smooth skin from my afternoon shave. She kissed the corner of my mouth, breathing frantically underneath me.

I wanted more.

I wanted it at all.

Titan found her restraint first and ended the kiss abruptly. She tilted her head down, her breaths still coming out shaky. Her hands loosened against my body and gently slid down my arms to the crook of my elbows.

I knew this was over.

If we continued much longer, we would be caught.

There was nothing to say. We obviously had a powerful connection, a physical combustion that rivaled the most powerful engine in the world. Our chemistry was unusual because it was so explosive. She wanted me, and I wanted her. I was drunk on her confidence, and she wanted to make love to my power. We were two sides of the same coin, two conquerors that wanted the same piece of land.

And neither one of us was willing to give in to the other.

I stepped back and wiped the corner of my lip, feeling her kiss still lingering on my skin. I gave her one final look before I stepped away, knowing there was nothing more to say. Anytime we were alone together, this would probably happen. Our minds were both so logical, both so hard, that we knew it was wrong.

But our bodies thought otherwise.

———

RAINDROPS SPLATTERED against my window that Tuesday afternoon. The light tapping was soothing as I sat at my desk and managed all my frontiers at once. I'd had a meeting that morning that wasn't as productive as I hoped it would be, but at least it was a step in the right direction.

Something about the rain put me at ease. Like

white noise that blocked out the sounds you didn't want to hear, the rain sheathed me from the cacophony and chaos of the city. If I hadn't had that meeting today, I probably wouldn't have come to work at all. I would have stayed in my penthouse and worked from home in front of the fireplace.

Natalie tapped her knuckles against my wooden door before she poked her head inside. "Sir, Ms. Titan is here to see you."

I nearly did a double take.

"She's not on your schedule for the afternoon. Shall I send her away?"

I had a meeting with my financial advisor, but that could wait until another day. "No. Clear my schedule for the next hour."

"Okay, sir."

"And don't disturb us."

Natalia gave a quick nod before she walked out.

I didn't know what Titan wanted, but I hoped it was something unprofessional.

Titan walked inside a moment later, a long, black rain jacket covering her dress underneath. She was in her usual stilettos, solid black and sleek. There wasn't a single scuff mark on them, as if they were brand new.

They probably were, actually.

I didn't rise from my chair, watching her like a hawk watched its prey. Now she was in my world, on my turf. This was my kingdom, and she was a mere citizen now. I was the king, and she was a simple subject.

She sat down in the leather armchair facing my desk and immediately crossed her legs. "Thanks for seeing me, Hunt."

"Pleasure is all mine." My arms rested on the armrests of my chair, and my leg was crossed, one ankle resting on the opposite knee. My fingertips felt the wooden armrest underneath me, drawing intricate circles. My office was a direct contrast to hers. I preferred rich and dark colors, bold aesthetics that matched the testosterone running through my veins. It was a powerful place, a home where most of my ideas were born.

Titan sat in an elegant position, her back rigid and straight but the features of her face soft. Her hair was down that afternoon, her dark strands acting as a curtain around the back of her head. It reached down her shoulders and past her gorgeous tits. She didn't bring a bag with her or a folder. Whatever she wanted to discuss would only be conveyed verbally.

That was a good sign.

"How can I help you, Titan?" As with any

business meeting, I didn't voice my assumptions before the other party stated their demands. I suspected I knew why she was there, but I wasn't going to throw my hat in the ring just yet.

"I wanted to know if you'd reconsidered my offer."

There was only one offer she'd made, so I assumed she wasn't talking about anything else. "There's nothing to reconsider." Based on her requirements, it wasn't something I could do long term. Even short term might be a struggle. There were times when I wanted to fuck her hard and fast, taking her in whatever position I desired. I didn't want to have to ask permission. And I certainly didn't want to be given it either.

She tilted her head slightly, absorbing my simple remark without offense. "Then that's a firm no?"

All I gave was a nod.

"Care to elaborate?"

My hands gripped the edges of my chair because I loved the shade of her lipstick. I wanted to stand in front of her, sweep her hair into my hand, and plow my enormous cock inside that slender little throat.

I wanted to make her gag.

"I'm too dominant. We both know that."

"But you don't always need to be dominant."

"If that's the case, why don't we switch?"

She pressed her lips together tightly, lacking a counterargument.

"I think it'd be a lot of fun, Titan. Having a woman like you take charge would be sexy as hell. But only for so long."

"I never said it had to be permanent."

"I'm thinking a week."

"That's not long enough for us to trust each other."

I shrugged in response.

She uncrossed her legs and continued to watch me, her thoughts swirling behind those intelligent eyes. Something was at work. Cogs were turning, and her mechanism was ticking. She suddenly rose to her feet, standing with perfect posture in front of my desk. "Let me show you what it could be like." Her hands went to the front of her jacket, and she slowly undid each button. "You might change your mind."

In record speed, I popped a boner.

When the last button was undone, she pushed the jacket off her shoulders, revealing her standing in a one-piece teddy made of sheer lace that covered some of her body and didn't leave much to the imagination.

Fuck.

A clasp was located near her crotch, telling me her lingerie could be crotchless with the snap of two fingers. The lace stretched over her body because it was perfectly formfitting, and her nipples were noticeable in the thin fabric.

Fuck. Fuck. Fuck.

She sauntered around my desk, changing my office into another one of her properties. Now she owned the building, owned the office, and owned me. She grabbed the two armrests of my chair and rolled me back until I was closer to the window. She immediately straddled my hips, palmed the back of my head, and then tilted my mouth to hers.

I was already lost in a haze, not thinking twice about what I was doing. My cock pressed against my slacks as it tried to get out and slip inside her. My hands glided to her thighs, squeezing the thin muscles under my grasp.

She gripped my tie and loosened it in seconds, kissing me at the same time. She pulled it from around my neck, sliding it down my shirt until it was wrapped around her fist. Then she grabbed my hands and pinned them around the back of my chair.

I let her overpower me, aroused by this beautiful woman who didn't hesitate to take action. She slowly ground against my cock, giving me friction while doing the same to herself. She brushed her lips against mine, teasing me as she secured my wrists together in an impressive knot. When I tugged against it, my hands could barely move.

This woman meant business.

Her mouth returned to mine, devouring my lips and tongue like they belonged to her exclusively. Her fingers undid the buttons of my shirt, and she kissed me, infused me with her passion. She was featherlight on top of me, but she exerted so much power that I could feel her everywhere.

I nibbled on her bottom lip, taking her mouth more aggressively than she took mine. I craned my neck to get to her, to have more of her. My tongue swiped into her mouth then slowly danced with hers.

She moaned.

"Titan…" I spoke into her mouth as I looked her in the eye, feeling my skin prickle everywhere. I wasn't even inside her yet, and I wanted to burst. My hands yanked against the silk of my tie, anxious to break free and enjoy her gorgeous body, but the knot was too strong.

Titan was too strong.

She pushed my shirt open to reveal my bare chest then undid my pants next. She yanked the belt out and tossed it on the floor before she unfastened the button and zipper. After some adjusting, she got my boxer briefs down to my ankles.

My mouth could lie to her and say it wasn't into this, but my throbbing cock couldn't. It was pumped with blood, so thick it was about to explode. I was slightly longer than I usually was because I was that hard up, that aroused by this woman. My balls were tight, anxious to give her my come anywhere she would take it.

She slid to the floor, her knees on the hard wood. Her face was close to my waist, her mouth looking beautiful that close to my cock. She hadn't sucked me off yet, and I was finally about to get that lipstick smeared against my cock.

I could barely breathe.

She ran her hand up my muscular thighs, slowly inching to my stomach. She massaged me gently, teasing me by not touching the one place I wanted to be touched the most. She eyed my big dick before she licked her lips.

Jesus Christ, woman.

She scooted closer to me, her lips parted and her eyes anxious.

I yanked on my hands again, wanting to grab her by the hair and guide her mouth to where I wanted her most.

She ran her hand through her hair and pulled it over one shoulder before she licked her lips again.

God.

She finally leaned down and pressed her mouth against my balls, my aching sac. She kissed the sensitive web of nerves before she dragged her soft tongue over my textured skin, making my balls tense so hard I actually forgot to breathe.

I tugged on my tie again.

She moved quicker, dragging her tongue everywhere. She sucked the skin into her mouth, getting more of it as she sucked harder. Her tongue moved across it, lubricating my balls with her saliva.

I'd never seen a woman give head like this. She took her time, dragged it out. She made me build up without even touching my dick. She pleased me like it was her profession—and she was the employee of the year.

I was tied to my chair in the middle of the day, rain hitting the windows, and the richest woman in the world was on her knees licking my balls like she couldn't get enough of them into her mouth.

Hottest thing I'd ever seen.

My dick couldn't be any harder.

She finally dragged her tongue all the way up my length, slowly rising until she reached the head of my cock. Now she held herself up on her knees, leaning over me with her perfectly styled hair across my stomach. She swiped her tongue over the head of my cock, tasting the pre-come that formed the second her mouth was on my balls.

She sheathed me all the way to my hilt.

"Fuck…" I ground my teeth together, but that didn't stop the moan from escaping my lips. My jaw was clenched so tightly it was about to pop. Her mouth was soft and warm, her saliva coating me all the way down.

She dug her nails into my bottom abs as she worked her neck to take my cock over and over. She kept her pace slow, gradually descending to my balls then back up again. When she pulled my head out of her mouth, a trail of saliva connected my cock and her lips to each other. She licked it with her tongue, severing the contact. Then she locked her gaze with mine.

And licked her lips.

My cock twitched in response. She placed a loving kiss on the tip of my dick then dragged her tongue along the groove. When she pushed him into the back of her throat again, she took him all the way. I was a big man with a big package, and I was used to women taking me in halfway because I was simply too long.

But I wasn't too long for Tatum Titan.

She sucked me off for another minute before she wrapped her hand around my base. She jerked me off slowly, squeezing and twisting her hand as she moved up and down. She locked her gaze on me, maintaining eye contact as she pleased me. "You don't come until I tell you to come."

My cock twitched in her hands.

"Do you understand?" She rubbed her thumb across the head, catching another drop of pre-come. She brought her thumb to her mouth and sucked it.

Every muscle in my body was tight in anticipation. I held her gaze, my breathing slowly escalating.

"Hunt." Her hand moved to my balls, and she massaged them before she dragged her tongue up my length.

This was the best fucking head I'd ever gotten.

Five-star blow job.

Made me forget every woman who'd ever wrapped her lips around my length.

Jesus Christ.

"Do you understand me?" She spoke with her mouth against the length of my cock.

She knew I wasn't going to come, but she wanted my cooperation. She wanted me to yield to her, to answer her when she asked a question. It was a preliminary to what was coming next.

But I wasn't hers to command, so I said nothing.

She rose to her feet and unsnapped the bottom of her teddy, opening herself up so she could take me without removing her lingerie. "Then I'll make you understand, Hunt."

I automatically tugged on my tie, my cock so thick it actually hurt. I'd never seen a sexier woman in my life, someone so confident in her skin. I watched her rip into a packet and roll the condom to the base of my dick.

Then she climbed on top of me, pointed my fat cock at her entrance, and slid all the way down.

I pressed my forehead to hers and groaned, doing my best to remain quiet so my assistants wouldn't know I was having the best sex of my life right now. My hips immediately flexed upward, shoving my length as deep inside her as I could go.

She wrapped her arms around my neck, adjusted herself until the bottoms of her feet were flat against the chair, and then she raised her body with perfect posture, holding herself upright without expressing the slightest exertion. Then she moved down again.

Fuck. Yes.

She kept her eyes on me, the fierce authority burning in her gaze. Her lips were parted as she breathed through her movement, riding my dick all the way from the tip down to the base. "Hunt...so good."

"Titan..." I tried to slip my hands out of the knot because now I was desperate to touch her, to feel that gorgeous body that was riding my dick.

"I love your cock."

I tugged again, using all of my strength to try to rip the tie in half. I didn't care if I went the rest of the day in just my collared shirt. My hands ached to touch this woman, to fuck her with my hands. "I love your pussy."

She took her time riding me, giving me slow and even strokes. When it was slow like this, it was just as good as a rough pounding. We took our time enjoying each other, my hips moving slowly to meet her thrusts.

I could do this all fucking day.

Natalie's voice came over the intercom. "Sir, I have Pine Rosenthal on the phone."

Goddammit, Pine.

Titan dug her nails into my shoulders. "You don't speak to anyone until I'm finished with you." She sat on my dick, taking in every single inch as she leaned back and hit the button on the intercom.

I couldn't barely think when I was buried this deep inside Titan's pussy. "Tell him I'll call him back. Don't disturb me for any reason."

Titan came back to me, fucking me like there had been no interruption at all.

I craned my neck so I could kiss her, stick my tongue in her mouth. I sucked her lips, kissed her mouth, and gave her my tongue as she gave me hers. I'd never fallen so deep into sex, had all of my surroundings fade away until there was nothing but the two of us. The experience was spiritual, existing on a different plane that was higher than reality.

So fucking good.

She rocked her hips forward and backward, grinding her clit against my pelvic bone. "I'm gonna come…all over this fat cock."

I closed my eyes for an instant, a moan escaping between my teeth.

She rocked harder, her breaths turning into whimpers. Her nails almost drew blood as she gripped me, nearly slicing me. She bit her bottom lip as her eyes focused on me, that beautiful blush in her cheeks just before she slipped off the cliff. "God…Hunt…yes."

I'd never struggled so hard not to come. I wanted to fill that condom with all of my seed, but I forced myself to wait. I watched her performance, the way her head rolled back as she suppressed the scream she wanted to release. Her pussy tightened around my cock, gripping it like a hand made of steel.

I breathed through my pleasure, my cock so thick it wasn't going to last much longer.

Her orgasm seemed to stretch on forever. Maybe it just seemed long because I was so anxious to follow her. Watching this woman enjoy my body was better than any porn I'd ever viewed.

She pressed her face into my neck as she finished, her screams muffled by my skin. She caught her breath before she sat back, back on top of my dick. "I'm gonna let you come…only because I know you have work to do."

I thrust my hips into her.

"Since you did as I asked, I'll reward you. How do you want it, Hunt? Slow and deep like this? Or hard and fast?"

I was so desperate to come I didn't care about anything else at that point. I just wanted to experience what she had felt, to feel that all-consuming orgasm that made her toes curl. "Hard and fast, Titan."

She planted her hands against my chest and got to work, moving up and down and taking my length at an incredible speed. The chair squeaked slightly from the momentum of her movements, her body shifting up and down, her pussy so wet there was hardly any friction.

I watched her tits shake and felt my cock harden to the breaking point. I breathed harder and harder, my hands tugging on the tie until it finally started to slip with my sweat. When my entire body stiffened, I stopped breathing, and with my balls pulled tightly against my body, I came.

And I came hard.

"Fuck…" The explosion was unreal. Like waves in an ocean storm, it was powerful and natural. I felt like a man, pure male pumped with nothing but testosterone. She fulfilled a fantasy I didn't know I had, making me come with such masculinity that it allowed my orgasm to stretch on a little longer than it normally would.

It was the best orgasm I'd ever had, the most powerful one to date.

It was unbelievable.

This woman was unbelievable.

My mind liquefied into melted butter, and I couldn't think clearly. I pressed my forehead to hers and gave her a soft kiss on the mouth. My cock softened inside her, but I didn't want her to leave. I didn't want to sever this connection we had. It was one of the rare times in my life when I actually felt something. My life wasn't mundane, ordinary, and blurry.

It was as clear as a sunny day.

She pulled off of me, fastened her crotch, and pulled on her jacket like we'd just come to an agreement about a business venture. "Think it over, Hunt." She fixed her hair and makeup, adopting her executive look and erasing the I-just-got-fucked-good look. Then she turned to the door.

"Are you gonna untie me?" My hands were still tied behind my back, my shirt was wide open, and my cock lay against my stomach, the tip of the condom full of all the seed I just gave her.

She rested one hand on the steel handle as she looked at me. "I'm sure you can handle it."

THIRTEEN

Tatum

I WALKED INTO THE BOOKSTORE AND BROWSED THE sections on the shelves. People stood in corners with open books in their hands, browsing through the pages like it was a library, something they could take for free.

Others were in the café, drinking coffee while they worked on schoolwork. Most of the people were young, going to college to get that dream job they would never find. I owned this bookstore, but this was only the second time I'd been inside.

I arrived at the poetry section and searched until I found the hardback I was looking for.

THE MIGHTY OAK
A Collection of Poems

T. Titan

I STARED at the book in my hands, feeling a lifetime of memories in something I'd already read a hundred times. I had the original still sitting in my desk. I had more than one copy, but yet, I felt the need to buy another every so often.

The whole reason why I owned a dying business was just to have this.

And to share it with the world.

I went to the register and paid for it before I placed it in my bag.

Thorn called me. "Hey, sweetheart."

"Hey." I released a quiet sigh that I doubted he could hear.

"What's got you down?"

"Nothing."

Silence.

"I'm at the bookstore…"

That was all Thorn needed to know. "Isa and I are getting dinner at CUT. You wanna join us?"

"You know I do."

"We're getting a table now. See you soon."

"Okay." I hung up and found my driver parked at the sidewalk. He immediately hopped out of the driver's seat and opened the back door so I could get inside. Then he shut it behind me before he took me to my next destination.

Sometimes I was in the mood to be taken around, to have someone else worry about traffic and pedestrians. Other times, usually late at night, I liked to take my own car out for a spin.

Somewhere I could test the engine.

I arrived at the building, took the elevator to the top floor, and then arrived on the terrace where the restaurant was. Glass walls were erected around the tables, protecting everyone from the cold wind that traveled along the skyscrapers of the city. Heated lamps kept everyone warm as they sat together at tables with white tablecloths and dimly lit candles.

I found Isa and Thorn and took a seat. "I'm starving."

Thorn pushed the basket of bread toward me.

I took a slice and gently buttered it with my knife. I didn't eat bread much, steering clear of carbs in any capacity. Thorn was the same way, but he had a lot more willpower. I indulged here and there, knowing life was too short not to feast once in a while.

"Anything new with Hunt?"

I finished chewing my piece of bread before I

VICTORIA QUINN

wiped the corner of my mouth. "A few things, actually."

"This should be good," Thorn said. "You'll wear him down eventually."

"I stopped by his office…" I told them everything that happened, skipping the detailed parts so they wouldn't lose their appetites.

"Wow." Isa shook her head. "My god, that's hot."

Thorn waved at his face. "I'm a little warm."

"That'll change his mind." Isa snapped her fingers. "Give it a day."

It'd been a few days, actually. I knew he enjoyed it because I could feel how thick he was inside me. He was pulsing, about to explode. "I'm not too sure. Hunt is a little harder than most men. His backbone is made of steel."

"But he has a dick." Thorn drank his wine. "Don't give him too much credit."

"True," Isa said. "And if he doesn't cave, just make another move."

"You'll change his tune eventually," Thorn said. "It's not every day a woman like you walks into his office and ties him up."

I could never tell anyone outside the four of us what I did in my private time. Fortunately, they were all just as kinky as I was, so it wasn't surprising. They

194

had their own fetishes, their own desires. I wasn't the only oddball in the world.

"Maybe you should contact him," Isa suggested.

"No," I said quickly. "I already put myself on the table. The ball is in his court now."

Thorn nodded in approval. "Attagirl."

"You think he's trustworthy?" Isa asked.

"I do." Thorn swirled his glass before he took a drink. "He keeps his head low. You can tell he's a man with his own secrets. He wants to stay off the radar, and he respects anyone who wants the same."

"Have you spoken to him?" Isa asked. "You don't even know him."

"I just know these things," Thorn said vaguely. "I'm good at reading people."

"What kind of secrets does he have?" Isa asked.

"Who says he has secrets at all?" I asked. "He seems pretty open."

"No, she's right," Thorn said. "Everyone has secrets. I know he's had an estrangement with his father for the past seven years. They haven't spoken to each other once."

That was news to me. "Why?"

Thorn shrugged. "Something to do with business, I think."

"Is his father wealthy?" When I'd looked into

Hunt, I'd concentrated on his presence in the media. While he was a person of interest, he kept his personal life out of the headlines. He was only pegged as a player, but that was pretty normal for a rich and a handsome man like him. I didn't dig into his personal history.

"Very," Thorn said. "That's where Hunt got most of his money."

"I didn't know that…" Hunt didn't seem like the kind of man who did business with anyone. I was surprised he stepped on his father's shoulders to get where he is now.

"He took that money and turned it into something else," Thorn said. "I've heard his father expected to take a certain percentage of his profits because he helped Hunt in the beginning, but Hunt refused. I think there's more to the story, but it goes something like that…"

"Interesting." I hadn't even had a chance to order my drink yet, and I was learning his autobiography.

"Maybe you can ask him about it when you get a chance," Thorn said. "Since you're a woman who always gets what she wants…I say he'll be yours eventually."

"We never talk about anything personal in my arrangements." I didn't want Hunt to know anything about me, and I didn't care enough to learn anything about him. That was the cold, hard truth. It was simpler that way, made it easier to go our separate ways.

Thorn shrugged. "Things come up when you least expect them."

———

I STILL DIDN'T hear anything from Hunt.

What game was he playing?

He liked the sex. There was no denying that. I liked it too—which was obvious. How could he not want more? How could he not take the bait off the line?

Was I missing something?

I thought I understood my opponent, but I started to wonder if I didn't understand him at all.

But I refused to reach out to him again. The second I did, I would lose the power. I already went out on a limb by stopping by his office and fucking him before I walked out. If I did something like that again, it would only push me down further.

But finally, he texted me. *Titan.*

I stared at my phone as I sat on the couch in my living room, wearing a t-shirt with panties underneath. I stared at the message before I opened it and sent a message in response. *Hunt.*

I'm stopping by in ten minutes.

If he wanted to meet face-to-face, maybe he had something good to say. Maybe he was ready to accept my offer and get started right away. When his hands were tied behind his back, I loved watching his muscular body work to break free. I loved seeing his massive shoulders clench tightly, the blood pounding in his big muscles. His jaw was clenched so tight I thought he might rip his jaw.

I was hot just thinking about it.

Ten minutes later, the elevator doors opened directly into my penthouse. He was in black jeans, a navy blue shirt, and a black jacket. He walked inside, carrying himself like he owned the building. He looked down at me on the couch like he was about to climb on top of me and fuck me right then and there.

I stood up, abandoning my Old Fashioned on the table, and walked up to him. I was in a long t-shirt and my thong, barefoot. He'd already seen me naked many times. I didn't see the point in getting dressed up when he only gave me ten minutes to prepare.

He didn't say anything, his eyes roaming over my body like it was the first time he'd seen me like this.

"Can I get you something to drink?"

"No. We can share." He closed the gap between us, and his hands circled my waist. He enclosed me in his big arms, his masculine jaw coming close to my mouth. When he breathed, I felt the air tickle my skin. He smelled of body wash, like he just got out of the shower not too long ago.

"I'm not the kind of woman who likes to share."

"You can make an exception—for me." He kissed the corner of my mouth, taking my breath away with the gentle touch.

I closed my eyes, the heat rushing over my skin.

He guided me to the couch, warning me of what would happen next.

I stood my ground and kept him back. "Are you here to accept my offer?" I whispered against his mouth. I didn't want to get carried away unless we'd decided on what our relationship was going to be. Because feeling him in my hands was driving me crazy. I wanted to push him back on the couch and have my way with him, to fuck him until I was too sore to walk.

Hunt brushed his thumb across my bottom lip as he looked at me with eyes the color of oil. "I'm here to negotiate."

"Negotiate?" I whispered. "What does that mean?"

He wore a slight smile. "You wouldn't know, huh?"

We stood in front of my fireplace, the flames filling the room and making us warm even though the tension was already scorching hot.

"I'm willing to accept your offer with a few stipulations."

"Such as?"

"We take turns. You're in charge one night. And then I'm in charge the next."

The very last thing I wanted was to submit to a man. When he said he had some terms he wanted to discuss, I thought he meant hard limits, things he wasn't comfortable doing, like whips and chains. Not completely twisting the arrangement around. "No. That's not what I want."

"Then you have it your way for the first half. Then, for the second half, I get my way. That's fair—even."

"No." I wasn't interested in being dominated, in being powerless to someone else. I'd already done that, and I didn't like it. I wouldn't like it now.

"No?" he asked.

"I'm in charge the entire time. You do what I say —no questions asked. When you said you wanted to negotiate, I thought you meant on small details. What you're asking now is a completely different offer than the one I made."

"You're right." He grabbed my chin and directed my face to him. "It's a compromise."

"I don't want to compromise—"

"I want you. You want me. As much as I would enjoy a repeat of the other day, I need more than that. If you want to own me the way you're asking, then I need to own you in return. That's the only way I'll agree. This has to be equal. This has to be a fair distribution of power. You want me to trust you? Then you need to trust me too."

As reasonable as his request was, it was appalling. I didn't want that kind of relationship. "No." I stepped back from him, his hand leaving my face in the process. "Take my offer as it stands, or don't take it at all."

His arms moved to his sides, the muscles of his biceps cut and rigid. "If you gave me a chance, you would like it. You've had me between your legs before. You can only imagine how incredible I'll make you feel…the kind of places I'll take you to."

It was appetizing, but unrealistic. "No."

When he cocked his head to the side, I knew I wasn't going to get a calm acceptance from him. "Why?"

"It doesn't matter why."

"It does to me. Trust works both ways. Tell me why you feel this way, and maybe I'll reconsider."

I wanted Hunt more than any other man in my life. There was something about him that pleased me, satisfied me, and soothed me all at the same time. Now I had a way to get him to take my offer, to accept my terms.

I just had to be honest.

Come clean.

Tell the truth.

And he would be mine.

His eyes were still glued to mine, waiting for an answer.

A part of me trusted him, felt like I could tell him anything. I could dig into my past and open the gates, along with everything that would come flooding out. But my better judgment, my cold heart, stopped me. "I can't tell you, Hunt."

His hands moved to my waist. "Why not?"

"Because I can't." I grabbed his wrists and gently pulled his arms off my body. "The reasons don't matter. I'm only looking for one thing from you. There's no need to exchange personal stories."

His eyes closed for just an instant before they reopened. "I haven't known you very long, Titan.

But you're an incredible woman, and I already consider you to be a friend. That may not mean much to you, but I don't have many friends...for a reason."

It did mean something to me, but that wasn't a good thing. I didn't want to feel anything at all. "I don't have many friends either."

"I know you have a few you keep in your inner circle."

"It took them many years to get there."

He stared me down, burning me with his gaze until I was forced to meet it. It was like the hot sun beating down on a clear day. You didn't want to look at it, but sometimes you couldn't help it. "Then I can't accept your offer, Titan. I'm willing to be what you want in a relationship, even if it goes against my principles, if you're willing to break your rules in the same way. Though if you won't make the same sacrifice but expect me to do it...then we have no deal."

Like a knife in the heart, I'd been gutted. All of my insides were spilling out, dropping on the floor of my living room. Men had come and gone, and I'd never blinked an eye over it. But hearing Hunt say no was like a fist to the face.

It took me a few seconds to recover.

Hunt sighed as he stared at me. "I don't want this to end either…"

"Just think about it longer—"

"No." His eyes were dark like the night just before dawn. "We're both in this together, or we aren't in this at all. You won't change your mind, and I respect that. But don't expect me to change mine."

I should have known he wouldn't say yes. A man that hard, that reputable, wouldn't change everything about himself for one woman—I wouldn't respect him if he did. "Okay…then this is it."

He nodded. "This is it."

———

AS THE DAYS PASSED, I waited to feel better.

I tried to forget about Diesel Hunt.

I prayed I'd forget about him.

But with every passing day, I didn't get any better.

In fact, I just got worse.

Men had turned down my offer before. Not many, but some. There was never any disappointment. I just went out and found someone to replace them. It had always worked up until that point.

But Hunt was different.

I actually liked the guy.

Maybe it was best that it didn't work out. If I liked him now, sleeping with him for a few months wouldn't help matters. I'd never struggled to keep my feelings platonic, but when I actually considered telling him about who I really was, I knew Hunt had gotten under my skin.

He lived under my skin.

I owned ten cars. My Bugatti was in the parking garage of my building because I loved to drive that thing everywhere. I had a few other cars in storage lots, at my house in Rhode Island, and few others in California.

I loved cars.

It was my weakness, buying a beautiful engine that had the kind of horsepower that could tug a tree stump from the ground—without breaking a sweat. I loved the sleek shine of the paint, the aerodynamics that made it cruise at 150 miles per hour but still feel like sixty-five. I loved that kind of power in my fingertips, the adrenaline coursing through the engine as well as my veins.

I decided the best way to forget about Hunt was to go shopping.

For a new ride.

Brett Maxwell owned some of the most luxurious cars in the world. They were rare because they were pricey, and they took a long time to make. Each one was a sample of perfection, the kind of design that made anyone who appreciated cars swoon.

I walked into the dealership in my pencil skirt and heels and browsed the models on the floor. The fastest edition they made was the Maxwell Bullet, which contained two V6 engines and a shit-ton of horsepower. With leather seats, state-of-the-art sound system, and rims that shone brighter than my jewels, it was the car for me.

And I knew I wanted it in black.

A salesman approached me, a man in his fifties. He looked me up and down with uncertainty, like there was no way a thirty-year-old woman seriously could be looking for a car. "Good afternoon, ma'am. Can I help you with something?"

"I'm just taking a look around." I eyed the Bullet right in front of me. "Beautiful."

"They are," he said in agreement. "Are you browsing for your boss?"

He probably thought I was a secretary. Apparently, it was impossible that a pretty woman could be anything but an assistant. "Sort of. I'm my own boss, so I'm browsing for myself."

"Ohh…that's wonderful. We have some older models out back. Would you like to see those?"

Instead of rolling my eyes, I forced a smile. "Actually—"

"Ms. Titan." Brett Maxwell himself appeared out of his office. In a midnight black suit, a powerful physique underneath like the engine in this car, and a charming smile, he walked up to me and extended his hand. "Such a pleasure having you in today."

I shook his hand. "Nice to see you again, Mr. Maxwell."

"I assure you the pleasure is all mine." He wore the kind of smile that reached his eyes. He had a square jaw, a strong facial structure like the famous actors that walked the red carpet. He was older than me, but not by much. There was something about his eyes that felt familiar, like those very eyes had looked at me in a more intimate setting. "I could talk about my cars all day with anyone—especially a beautiful woman like yourself."

I smiled.

"There's nothing that would complement this car more than you in the driver's seat." He walked over to the front and opened the door. "If you do buy this car, I'm gonna have to snap a picture of you and blow it up into a poster—if you don't mind."

"Not at all." I took a seat behind the wheel, felt the leather interior, and examined the sound system.

It was a two-seater, but I didn't need any more room than that.

"Start this beauty."

I placed my foot on the brake and hit the button.

She came to life with a roar.

"Isn't that the most beautiful sound you've ever heard?"

Second to Hunt coming. "Yes."

He went over the other features of the car, telling me exactly what a vehicle like this was capable of. His excitement was obvious in his expression, discussing something he was truly passionate about. "Let me know if I'm boring you."

"You're fine, Mr. Maxwell."

"Brett." He took my hand and helped me out of the car. "Whether you buy a car or not, I'm hosting a race this weekend. Just going to be me and a few friends at my track on Saturday. It's where we take our cars for a spin, really push them to the limit. You're welcome to join."

I would love to pick up some speed outside the city. Maybe it would get my mind off the man I couldn't have. "I'll take your invitation—and the car."

He grinned. "You have no idea how happy that

makes me. The richest woman in the world driving my car…it's quite a compliment."

———

IN SKINTIGHT DENIM jeans and black racing shoes, I drove to Maxwell's property outside the city in Connecticut. I wore a red leather jacket, my hair gently pulled from my face, with a few strands coming loose. My nails were painted deep red, complementing the jacket.

I loved my car.

It was powerful and fast, maneuvering around other cars with ease. I didn't have to slam my foot on the gas and wait a few seconds for the car to respond to my needs. It was a beast, purring at the challenge and taking off.

It was awesome.

I took the right turn and entered the exclusive property of Brett Maxwell. He had a mansion in the midst of green and trees, and behind it was his personal raceway. I followed the small road on his property until I reached the asphalt track miles away. Cars were circling the roadway, their engines loud as they sped by.

A dozen men stood off to the side, a sea of

parked cars surrounding them. There were Ferraris, Lamborghinis, and everything else I could think of. Someone else had a Maxwell car as well—but it was in red.

When I pulled to the spot at the end, everyone turned my way. The windows were tinted so they couldn't see my face. They probably assumed I was one of Brett's poker buddies, not a woman who shared the same appreciation for cars that they did. I killed the engine and stepped out.

They all stared.

I sauntered over to them, recognizing a few of the guys by face but not name. They were all in the billionaire club, owning companies around the world and all along the East Coast.

Brett stepped out of the crowd when he saw me. "My favorite client is here." He wore a handsome smile that showed all his teeth, and that happy expression looked so familiar. I was sure I'd seen it before, but I must not have. Otherwise, I'd be able to recall why I felt that way. He extended his hand.

I shook it.

"Your favorite client?" A man beside him asked incredulously. "I've bought two cars from you."

"And did you bring either of them today?" Brett

countered without looking at him. "Titan, do you need a helmet?"

"Please."

"I'll be right back." He walked to a tub near the racetrack and pulled out a sleek black helmet.

While I waited, I introduced myself to the men. Charles Brown was the founder of a high-end sports apparel brand, and Lance Washington was the owner of the New York Giants. Once I heard their names, I knew exactly what they were. All in their thirties, they were part of the young and rich club.

We made small talk until Brett returned with the helmet. "This is gonna look great on you."

"Thanks." I stuffed the helmet under my arm.

"Have you done this before?" Charles Brown asked. "Maybe you should ride with one of us for the first time."

Whenever someone assumed I couldn't do something, that only made me want to prove them wrong. Instead of showing my irritation and letting this man know he'd insulted me, I just smiled. "I can handle it."

Brett smiled at me. "You'll have to take me for a spin. I'm sure it'll be a wild ride."

Some men treated me as an equal the second we met. There were very few of them who did, but I always appreciated every single one. The rest of them couldn't process the fact that I was a woman who could do more than give birth.

Brett waved to someone across the pavement. "Hey, I want you to meet someone."

I looked in Brett's direction and saw a man in dark jeans and a black t-shirt. His cut arms were defined in the fabric, and his expansive chest looked muscular even though the bare skin couldn't be seen. His dark hair was the same shade as his eyes. He walked toward us, and his eyes locked on me.

Diesel Hunt.

Of course.

He ignored Brett as he joined our group, his eyes on me the entire time. No one else seemed to exist besides the two of us. When we were locked in an intimate connection like this, I couldn't stop thinking about the way his mouth tasted, the way the rest of his body felt against my lips.

Hunt stopped in front of me, getting closer to me than anyone else did.

"This is Tatum Titan," Brett explained. "If you don't recognize her face, I'm sure you recognize her name."

He glanced at the helmet tucked under my arm

before he looked at me again. "We've met." He extended his hand.

I stared at it, feeling strange for greeting him in a way that didn't justify just how intimate our relationship was. I finally slipped my small hand into his, feeling his fingers against my wrist. "How are you, Mr. Hunt?"

The corner of his lip hiked up at the way I addressed him. "Well. How about you, Ms. Titan?"

"I'm wonderful. I'm about to see how far I can push my new girl."

He glanced over my shoulder at the Bullet parked behind me. "She's beautiful. Can I meet her?"

"Sure." I guided Hunt away from the group and approached my black car. I hadn't locked the doors, so they were unlocked and accessible. I didn't touch the paint for fear of fingerprints, and he did the same. He walked around the car, his hands sliding into his pockets. "Black is always a good choice."

"It was love at first sight."

"Yeah?" he asked. "I didn't think you believed in that sort of thing."

"I didn't either—until I saw her."

"It's a her, huh?" That teasing smile stretched across his ridiculously handsome face. "Girl-on-girl action...pretty hot."

"If you think that's hot, you haven't seen nothing yet, Hunt."

His smile disappeared quicker than a snap of a finger. Now he stared at me like a hunter about to pin down his prey. It was the same look he'd given me in the hallway at the charity gala. He'd pinned me to the wall and devoured me like he had every right to do whatever he wanted.

I still wanted him to say yes.

"Come with me." He nodded in the opposite direction before he crossed the pavement to the other side of the track. "Let me introduce you to my woman."

I eyed the red paint, a smile forming on my lips. "You have one of your own."

"Just got her a few weeks ago—haven't broken her in yet."

"She's lovely. And I like the red."

"I like the black." He stood beside it with his hands in his pockets. The conversation died away, and all we did was stare at each other. Our last conversation had ended with a finality, and we'd gone our separate ways in life. But now that we were together again, the same heated intensity built between us. I was undressing him with my eyes, and he was already fucking me in the back of his mind.

"I'm gonna race some of the guys. You better put your money on me."

"My money is always on you, Titan." He stepped toward me, getting so close that people would accurately assume we were more than just friends. "Be careful. Sometimes people get out of hand at these things."

"I'll be fine, Hunt." I turned away.

He grabbed my wrist and steered me back toward him. The authority in his eyes stopped me from questioning him. "I mean it. Be safe."

"Thank you for your concern, but I don't need it."

He released me, but reluctantly.

"You wanna race me, sweetheart?" Charles asked from beside Brett.

There was nothing I hated more than being called that, especially in a condescending way. Men were constantly belittling me without even realizing what they were doing. "Sure. But let's make it interesting."

"Ooh," Brett said. "How much are we putting on the table?"

"If I win," I said. "You never call me sweetheart again."

Charles's eyes widened with surprise.

"If you win, I owe you a million."

Hunt came to the circle, his arms across his chest.

Charles continued to stare at me incredulously. "You're being serious?"

"Dead serious." I extended my hand to shake on the bet.

He shook his head like he still couldn't believe it then took my hand. "I'll gladly take your money, Titan."

"We'll see about that…" I walked to my car and secured my helmet on my head. When I got to the door, I turned around to look at my opponent.

Hunt had him gripped by the arm, and he said something directly into his ear.

Charles's expression was blank, his face pale. When Hunt released him, he stepped back and didn't make eye contact again.

I didn't know what he said, but I suspected it had something to do with me.

————

THE LIGHT CHANGED from red to yellow, and when it hit green, we both slammed our feet on the gas.

And we were off.

I'd driven my Bullet throughout the week, taking

nighttime adventures through the city and into the countryside. I'd tested her engine, her brakes, and her stability. I could take turns sharper than I thought possible and hardly shifted in my chair.

I had this in the bag.

Charles was in a Ferrari, a beautiful car that deserved my respect. It was yellow and shiny, the paint job still brand-new. His engine was loud even to my ears.

I gained more momentum than he did on the straightaway, inching past him. I was on the right side, and I had to maneuver to the left, cutting him off so I could hug the center of the circle.

But he wasn't going to let that happen.

When we approached the turn, he was still going fast, refusing to slow down.

That was a mistake.

I tapped the brake lightly with my foot, allowing him to pass me in the turn. But his wheels lost traction for a second, smoke from his ties coming up into the air. The event was enough to make his car veer slightly to the right.

I hit the gas halfway through the turn, gripped the steering wheel so I wouldn't lose control, and sped in the small gap between him and the edge of the line. If he wanted his spot back, he would have to hit me.

And he better not touch my car.

I gained momentum quicker than he did, my tires unaffected by the deep turn. I got an advantage on him, and before I knew it, we were at the next turn.

Despite his mistakes last time, he didn't slow down. He kept going, hoping to round me in the corner. He turned his wheel in my direction to keep a steady grip.

I didn't slow down either, knowing he would gain on me if I did.

I could spin out. My tires could lose traction. Hunt's warning came into my mind.

But I ignored all of that.

I hit the gas harder, made it through the turn, and crossed the finish line half a second before he did.

I got to keep my money—and my respect.

I slowed the car down then drove off the racetrack, parking my car where I'd initially left it when I arrived. Some of his Charles's friends met him at his car, but everyone else came to me the second I opened the door.

Brett was the first one to pat me on the shoulder. "Worth every penny, right?"

"She is, Brett."

He laughed then wrapped his arm around my shoulder. "Hunt, get a picture of us."

Hunt pulled out his phone, looking annoyed with that stern expression on his face, and then snapped a few pictures.

"Thanks, man," Brett said.

Hunt only nodded.

"Where did you learn to drive like that?" Brett asked.

I shrugged. "Just here and there…" Truthfully, I'd never been on a racetrack before. My only experience had been watching NASCAR on TV. "I've always loved cars. Have a deep affection for them."

"I can tell," Brett said. "That's why you and I get along so well." He stood beside Hunt and tapped the back of his wrist against his arm. "She's got some serious moves, huh?"

Hunt nodded.

Seeing them side by side made me realize how similar they were. They both had square jaws, eyes the same color as my Bullet, and a similar build and height. My eyes shifted back and forth between them, taking in the features that were too similar to be a coincidence.

"I'm gonna give Charles a pat on the back," Brett

said. "You know, for trying." He walked off, leaving Hunt and me alone together.

Hunt's expression didn't change, just as hard as it'd been a moment ago. He didn't congratulate me on the win or seem remotely impressed.

I knew exactly what he was thinking. "I'm still in one piece."

"No need to be reckless."

"I wasn't reckless."

"I disagree. I saw what you did in that turn there."

I didn't like being berated, being told I was wrong. "You aren't my boyfriend, Hunt."

"But I'm your friend," he said coldly. "Friends look out for each other."

Friendship was sacred to me. It was a beautiful relationship between two people who didn't need anything from each other—they just cared for one another. It was very rare in life for me to meet someone that I liked and trusted. If I considered you to be a friend of mine, then you were exceptional—and very close to my heart. Being friends with Hunt was far more meaningful than it seemed on the surface. "What did you say to Charles?'"

"Nothing worth mentioning."

I stepped forward. "Hunt." Making a demand of

Hunt wouldn't make him cooperate. He was just as stubborn as I was, unyielding. He only gave an answer because he wanted to give an answer.

"I'd break all of his bones if he even came close to touching one of yours."

———

I WALKED into my penthouse and pulled off my leather jacket. I'd said goodbye to everyone at the racetrack before I got into my car and took off.

Hunt didn't say anything to me.

A part of me expected something to happen between us, that he would ask me to come over. But since we both knew nothing could happen anyway, we just went our separate ways.

That didn't stop me from being disappointed.

Just when I slipped off my shoes, the buzzer from the elevator went off.

My heart jumped into my throat. My pulse throbbed in my neck. The air stopped in my lungs because my body shut down for a split second. Time stood still as my mind traveled to the man I thought about constantly.

Was Hunt the one buzzing for me?

I pressed my forefinger to the button. "Titan."

His deep voice sounded through the speaker, so masculine it was unmistakable. "It's me."

I knew exactly who *me* was. I hit the button and allowed the elevator to rise to my floor. While I waited, my pulse quickened in my veins. I was so aroused by the thought of him stopping by. When we went our separate ways, neither one of us stopped thinking about the other.

Like two magnets, we were constantly being pulled together by an invisible force we couldn't see—only feel. I watched the numbers on the elevator escalate the closer he came to my floor. He was just two floors below mine when I swallowed, my throat suddenly feeling dry and my tongue feeling swollen. I pictured his naked body on top of mine, thrusting so deep inside me my body convulsed.

The numbers finally stopped, there was a quiet ding, and then the doors opened.

Hunt stood in the center, looking just as appetizing as he did earlier in his black t-shirt and dark jeans. He slowly walked inside, the elevator doors staying open until he was finally out of the way.

I controlled my breathing so it wasn't so obvious that I was excited, but the flush of my fair skin was a dead giveaway. The desire in my eyes was practically a billboard, a sign covered with bright colors and neon lights.

He stood right in front of me, looking down into my face like a lion about to pounce. He walked into my penthouse like his was the name on the deed. He even stared at me like I was his property even though he had no such claim over me. This man wanted to own this city as much as I did—but he also wanted to own me.

I should have asked him what he was doing there, but I already knew the answer. I should have told him to leave, that I wasn't going to compromise on my decision, but my mouth stayed glued shut.

His hand moved to my neck, his large fingers possessing the hold of a quarterback. He slowly slid them up my neck, taking a short break over my pulse, and then cupped the back of my head. He moved his mouth to mine and took exactly what he wanted.

Me.

His arm circled my waist, moving all the way around until his hand gripped the opposite side of my waist. His powerful body pressed against mine, every inch of hard muscle acting as bricks in a skyscraper. His mouth moved with mine leisurely, every kiss slow and purposeful. He didn't kiss me aggressively like he did the other day. Now it was slow and steady, his lips doing all the work while his tongue stayed back.

When my hands overcame the shock of his embrace, they explored his chest. I loved the intricate lines of muscle of his body. A man didn't look this good unless he hit the gym every day and ate his meat and vegetables. He was so cut, he could be an underwear model on a billboard in New York City, and cars would crash in the road since no one would be paying attention to what they were doing.

He squeezed me to his chest and released a quiet moan directly into my mouth.

Damn, so sexy.

Now I didn't care about our conflicts of interest. I didn't care about our stalemate. Now I just wanted this man deep inside me, giving me his hard cock while his lips continued to devour mine.

Like we were of one mind, he scooped me up and held my body against his. My legs hooked around his waist, and I held my body up by his shoulders, carrying my own weight even though he could carry three of me.

He strode down the hall and found my bedroom even though he'd never been in there before. It was spacious, with a king bed with a cream-colored comforter and matching dressers. A gray rug was on the floor, a vase of lilies on the nightstand.

Hunt stripped my clothes off as he kissed me, kissing the rest of my body the same way as he kissed my lips. When I was naked, he pulled his shirt over his head and dropped his jeans and boxers.

He was beautiful.

He separated my thighs and placed his mouth between my legs, the scruff of his jaw rubbing against my soft skin. His mouth dominated my opening, licking my clit before sucking it into his mouth.

My back arched, and my hands dug into my hair, my breathing haywire because I couldn't stop moaning. I couldn't stop writhing. A man's face between my legs was my greatest weakness, and Hunt gave head better than anyone else ever had. He ate my pussy like he was starving.

Felt so good.

Hunt pulled away abruptly just when I felt my orgasm on the horizon. Like the sun peeking over the ocean, I could see the small rays before the actual sun was visible. I could even feel it in my bones.

He held himself on top of me, his lips gleaming from the arousal between my legs. His expression was hard, staring at me like he despised me. It was a look both full of hunger and violent urges. "Close your eyes."

Heartbeats passed as I looked into his eyes. My body still squirmed slightly underneath him, eager for him to be back in between my legs—where he belonged. But he wasn't mine to command. I didn't own him—not yet.

"Close." He brushed his lips past mine, teasing me. "Your." He kissed me, the taste of my arousal coming into my mouth. "Eyes." He gave me his tongue, swirling it with mine before he receded. "Now."

An innate part of me absorbed his words and obeyed, doing as he asked without thinking twice about it. My eyes closed, and I saw the darkness of my eyelids. I was more aware of his warm body on top of mine, the raging need between my legs. I desperately wanted his mouth again, his beard to rub against me.

"Keep them closed until I say otherwise." He shifted back down, moving between my legs and kissing me and my warm folds. He circled my nub with his tongue before he delved his tongue deep inside me, exploring my soaking channel.

God, I was gonna come.

So hard.

But before I could, he moved away.

"Hunt…" I kept my eyes closed, but I didn't hold back my groan. I begged him with just a single word, not ashamed to admit I wanted this man. I wanted him to finish what he started.

I heard him grab his jeans from the floor and knew he was fishing out a foil packet.

Good.

He came back to the bed and crawled on top of me again.

I kept my eyes closed, but my hands went to his chest, feeling those smooth muscles that were warm to the touch. I loved his body. I loved his strength. I didn't need a man to protect me, but I felt safe anytime he stood in the same room. Like nothing could hurt me, not now and not ever. I didn't have to put on a front, be the cold executive who constantly had to prove herself to be respected as much as her male peers.

I could just be me.

He grabbed my wrists and pinned them above my head. Then he hooked two metal handcuffs onto my wrists.

"What are you doing?" My eyes snapped open and I yanked my wrists away, but they were already secure. "Get these off of me—"

He pressed his mouth against mine. "Trust me." His lips moved with mine before he pulled away and looked me in the eye. "Come back to me." He kissed me harder, his hand moving into my hair.

His touch silenced me, his power making me feel safe, not challenged. He continued to kiss me before my body started to unwind again, relaxing and tightening in all the best ways.

When my mind was back in the haze, he moved between my legs again. "Close your eyes."

I did as he asked, falling into darkness.

He kissed me slowly then blew over my opening, my wet folds tingling with the sensation. He kissed my pussy just the way he kissed my mouth—and he was so damn good at it.

I was going to come just like this, with his tongue inside me.

He circled my clit harder, his arms resting on the opposite sides of my thighs. He sucked my lips into his mouth with more pressure, pushing me to the very edge.

I was about to come. I could feel it. "Hunt…yes."

"Not yet."

"Hunt…" I squeezed my thighs against his head.

"Not until I say." The more he kissed me, the more difficult it became. I was hovering right at the edge of the line, about to explode in a whirlwind of pleasure. My thighs started to shake, and my nipples were so hard they started to ache.

"Please…"

He pulled his mouth away and crawled back up my body. "You'll come when I say so." He ripped a foil packet and sheathed his length with the condom. My eyes were still closed, but I imagined all of it in my head, his muscles protruding as he held himself up on arm. The way his muscles rippled with every adjustment he made. When he was ready, his thighs separated mine, and he held himself over me, folding me so he could get the deepest angle possible.

Then he kissed me, softly.

I moaned into his mouth, so desperate for that cock.

"Look at me."

I opened my eyes and stared straight into the coffee-colored eyes that haunted my dreams. He stared at me like I was an army he was about to conquer, like I was a woman he was about to make his queen. He pushed his head inside me, sliding all the way through because my pussy was so wet. He didn't stop until he was balls deep.

"God…" I tugged on the metal handcuffs, forgetting I was restrained.

He buried himself inside me, sitting still as he absorbed my tightness. He pressed kisses along my neck before he moved to my tits. He sucked each nipple into his mouth, gently rubbing his teeth against each one. He pulled my skin hard into his mouth, hurting me just a tiny bit to make me whimper.

He dragged his tongue up the valley between my breasts before he positioned himself on top of me, our gazes locked on one another.

Then he thrust.

Hard.

My body shook with each movement, my tits shifting up as he rocked me. I craved the touch of his face with my fingers, the feel of his muscular back, but I was locked in place. I couldn't do anything, vulnerable to this man.

He pounded into me, his balls slapping against my ass over and over. His cock was so big that he stretched me in the process, making me fuller than any man before him. He was six feet and three inches of pure masculinity, the perfect male specimen.

Now I was going to come harder than I would have before. His cock always hit me in the right spot because he was so swollen. I was able to topple over the edge. I was almost there when I realized I'd stopped breathing.

"No."

I growled in protest.

"You come when I tell you to." He worked up a sweat moving inside me, his tight ass clenching hard with every thrust. Blood flooded his working muscles, and his jaw tightened as he exerted himself.

Hottest thing I'd ever seen.

"Hunt, I can't wait any longer…"

"You'll wait until I say so."

I clenched my jaw and writhed, yanking on the handcuffs that were made of solid steel. My ankles locked together at the small of his back, and I started to moan uncontrollably, battling my body to control itself.

Why was he torturing me like this?

He suddenly slowed down, his thrusts turning into long and even strokes. "Titan." He kissed me hard on the mouth, giving me his tongue. His movements slowed down even more, his cock so thick it was about to rip the condom. "Now, you can come."

The second the words were out of his mouth, my body turned into a white-hot ball of fire. My skin melted from the heat, and my body convulsed all on its own. My hips thrust forward by themselves, and I moaned uncontrollably. The metal cut into my wrists because I was so desperate to hold on to him. When I screamed, everything was incoherent. Sometimes, his name came out. And sometimes, I said things I couldn't even understand.

He came at the same time, releasing a quiet moan that was nothing like the loud yells I made. He fit himself entirely within me when he released, wanting as much of my pussy as he could get.

When we were both finished, we stayed close together, his cock softening and my channel relaxing.

I wished a condom weren't separating us. I wished it were just him—and his come.

His hands reached up and unlocked the cuffs, freeing my wrists without moving off of me. He kept his eyes on me, still aroused even though we both had had amazing climaxes. It was the best one I'd ever had. But then again, I said that every time I fucked Diesel Hunt. And I'd probably say it again the next time.

———

HE CLEANED off in the bathroom and helped himself to two glasses of water. He never pulled his clothes back on, fortunately. I got to watch that beautiful, tight ass as he walked across the floor barefoot. With a back perfectly straight, he had an inverted line of muscle on his flank. The tight muscles of his waist led up to a wide back packed with the strength of ten men combined together.

He handed me a glass before he sat beside me in bed, his back against the headboard. He crossed his ankles and pulled the sheet over his waist, hiding his soft cock that was still impressively long. I had a nice view of the city on his side of the bed. It was nothing but glass, revealing a skyline full of bright colors in the darkness. He watched it, drinking his water in comfort.

I drank mine, watching him instead of the view. His jaw tightened and shifted every time he took a drink, and the lazy look in his eyes deepened as he relaxed in my bedroom. His hard chest was a solid line to his stomach, his front as rigid as his back. His biceps bulged out, and he had slim forearms covered in muscular veins. I could stare at his body for hours, enjoying it like a sculpture in an art gallery.

The covers were tucked underneath each of my armpits, covering my chest and everything below. My once smooth hair was now a mess from writhing on the bed and his big hand fisting it. I wasn't much of a talker. I chose to think in silence, and I judged my friendships based on that comfort. If we could sit together and not feel the need to say anything, then I knew it was a good fit.

I knew we had the right chemistry.

Hunt sat beside me until he finished his glass of water. He set the empty glass on my white nightstand and finally turned his head in my direction, showing more of his profile than his face head on. "I hope I made you reconsider."

"Reconsider what?"

"Our arrangement."

I'd let him overpower me, but I'd been too hard up to fight it. I'd been thinking about Hunt all week. My thighs had been desperate to squeeze his waist every single day. I'd found myself clenching my thighs behind my desk at work. At this rate, I would have the most toned thighs in the world.

"Both ways are good, regardless of who's in charge."

I was surprised I let him handcuff me. More important, I was surprised I enjoyed it. "It's not what I want."

"Well, it's what I want." He turned his face forward again and looked out the window. "And it's more than fair."

"More than fair?" I asked quietly. "I came to you with a proposition. You decided to turn it around."

"Just like I would in any business meeting. If you're treating this in the same way, then you shouldn't expect me to do anything else. If you want to make this happen, you need to make a deal. You're asking for a hundred percent, but you need to accept fifty."

I didn't know what kind of deals he made, but I never expected anything so low.

"No one else has ever asked this of you?"

The men I approached were more than happy to be my plaything. They enjoyed it, enjoyed not being in charge for once. They respected my ability to make decisions, to give them fantasies they didn't know they had. I taught them so much about themselves, made them into stronger men once we went our separate ways. "No."

He grabbed my arm and slowly tugged me until I was on his side of the bed. He pulled me against his chest, tucking me into the crook between his arm and torso. His arm wrapped around my chest, and he pressed his lips against my hairline. "Titan."

I closed my eyes as I inhaled the scent of his body soap. It was mixed with the smell of sex, mixed with the smell of me. I wanted him to smell like this every day, to be covered with my kisses and the grooves of my tongue. I wanted women to walk into his office and know some other woman was rocking his world every night. "Yes?"

"Accept my terms."

My arm hooked around his stomach, and I looked out into the city, seeing the quiet cacophony right on my doorstep. I was on the top floor of one of the biggest skyscrapers in the world. I nearly owned this city, and in a few years, it would be mine.

He tilted his head down toward me. "Do you want me, Titan?"

I met his gaze, my hair falling back down my body. "Yes."

"Then take me as I am."

"I don't make exceptions for people."

"Make an exception for me." He ran his hand through my hair, fingering the soft strands until he reached my shoulder. "You know you're just gonna think about me when you're with someone else. And I'm going to think about you."

My spine prickled at his touch and his words. I didn't want another man inside me, not when I wanted Diesel Hunt so much. But bending the rules for one person caused me to question my character, to question the iron fist with which I ruled. "I'll think about it."

Hunt grazed his fingers down my arm until he reached my hand. His palm rested over mine, his fingers falling into the divides between my digits. "Thank you."

FOURTEEN

Hunt

———————

"DUDE, WHY DON'T YOU EVER WANT TO GO OUT with us?" Pine spoke to me over the speakerphone in my office.

"I went out with you last week."

"For, like, five minutes. Did I tell you these girls are models?" He paused as he waited for my reaction over the phone. "As in, swimsuit models."

I still didn't say a damn word.

"Italian swimsuit models. And they're only here this weekend before they head back to Milan."

"Sounds like you'll have a good time. But I've got a few meetings this weekend."

Pine didn't buy it. "Bullshit. No, you don't."

"You know my schedule now?"

"I know you always put everything on hold when it comes to fucking."

I was already fucking someone—hard. "I'll try to rearrange some stuff and let you know." I had to throw him a bone. Otherwise, he wouldn't stop pestering me.

"You better rearrange some stuff because Mike and I aren't taking no for an answer."

"What do you even need me for? You can fuck a girl without me."

"But there's three of them," he said. "Otherwise, one girl will be left out."

"Then don't let her feel left out." My meaning was crystal clear. Threesomes weren't much different from twosomes. Pine would know if he weren't too chickenshit to try it. I'd had two women trade off giving me a blow job, the saliva sticking between my dick and one of the girls' mouths. Then the other one licked it away before she went to town. That was the best head I'd ever gotten—until Titan. She wiped away all my favorite fantasies and wrote her name in red all over them.

"Are you seeing someone or something?" The question came out of nowhere, unexpected and surprising.

"No." I was free to do whatever I wanted because Titan and I hadn't settled on anything. But truth be told, I didn't want to be with another woman. It seemed pointless when I would just think about Titan the entire time.

"Whatever. Call me later." He hung up.

I hit the button when the line went dead. If Titan accepted my terms, which I suspected she would, I'd have to figure out a solution with Pine. If I saw her for months, it would be really obvious to my friends I was exclusive with someone. I wouldn't be able to hide it. Titan would have to allow me to share our secret with a select few people. It's not like they would tell anyone.

I had a lunch meeting with Brett Maxwell, so I left the office and met him at La Croix down the road. I didn't have a reservation and neither did he, but for two guys like us, that wasn't a problem. We bypassed the line and got to a table right away. We ordered wine and lunch before we got to talking.

"How's the car treating you?"

"Lovely," I said. "I've gotten nothing but compliments."

"My sales have skyrocketed since reporters have seen you drive it around."

"That's because of me—not the car." I grinned across the table at him, teasing him because it was one of my favorite hobbies.

"Nah. I think it's the car." He drank his wine then

VICTORIA QUINN

glanced around the restaurant. "Titan is something, isn't she?"

Out of nowhere, my adrenaline rose slightly. It was a gentle simmer, but it was there nonetheless. My eyes narrowed as I looked at Brett, interpreting his meeting subtly. I didn't own this woman, but it seemed like I did. "She's remarkable."

"You don't meet women like her every day. She's more intelligent than both of us put together. And damn, that woman knows how to drive. She's got class, you know? I admire that."

His praise seemed platonic, as one business-minded person complimenting another. "As do I."

"I was thinking of asking the two of you to do a commercial for me. The two of you in one of my Bullets driving along the Amalfi coast. It's every person's dream, to be the biggest power couple in the world."

My pulse quickened. I could feel it beat against the metal strap of my watch. "We aren't a couple."

"I'm aware." He grinned at me, his face classically handsome like mine. "You couldn't land a woman like that."

I suppressed my smile, but only barely.

"But that will sell. Sex sells."

"I doubt she would want to be associated with me in that way." In fact, I knew she wouldn't. Only her close friends knew she was fucking me. She didn't want to hint to the world that I was actually in her bed every night, handcuffed and being ridden like a stallion. "Perhaps each of us in different cars, racing along the coastline."

Brett nodded before a slow smile crept onto his lips. "I like that idea…I like it a lot."

"I'm interested if she is."

"I'll arrange a meeting with her, feel her out. I'm not sure how much her participation will cost."

"You probably can't afford mine either."

He shook his head but wore a grin at the same time. "I gave you a free car. You owe me, jackass."

"I thought that was a sponsorship."

"No. That was an older brother spoiling his younger brother." He held up his glass and winked.

I didn't stop the smile from stretching across my mouth. "Do I look like a man who needs to be spoiled?"

"It doesn't matter how much rich you are. I'm always gonna cut you a deal." He drank from his glass before he returned it to the table. "I'll let you know what Titan says. She doesn't need the money, but she might go for it. I can tell she genuinely loves the car."

"She does."

"And for a woman who already owns every luxury car in the world, that's saying something."

"She recognizes quality when she sees it." Including me. "Let me know when you hear from her."

"I will. So, what's new with you?"

"Not much. I just saw you on Saturday."

"Diesel Hunt lives life in the fast lane. We both know that."

The one interesting thing going on in my life couldn't be discussed. The fact that he knew Titan and respected her made everything more complicated. "I'm about to make an offer on a software company. The owner made a lot of stupid decisions, and his empire is crumbling underneath him. I want to seize it before someone else does."

"If you know about it, doesn't that mean others do too?"

"It's been pretty hush-hush."

"And I thought you cared more about starting companies rather than saving them?"

"I do," I answered. "But this instance is unique. I

also offered to buy Titan's publishing house, but she refused to listen to my offer."

"Refused?" A smile formed on his face the second I said the words. "Wow. That woman is ruthless."

"The company is dying, but she won't let it go."

"Why?"

"No idea."

"Well, I'm sure there's a reason. A woman like that doesn't make poor business decisions."

From where I was standing, it seemed like it. She was losing more money every quarter than she had during the previous one. All of her other holdings were mass successes, except this one. Nothing was adding up. "Whatever the reason is, it has nothing to do with money."

"Maybe she's predicting a change in the market and will reap the rewards then."

"There's always been a change in the market—and she's not adapting."

He finished his wine before he poured another glass. "Maybe we'll never know. Or maybe she just didn't want to sell to you. A lot of people don't like you. Can't blame her for feeling the same way."

"Everyone likes me," I countered. "Except you."

He chuckled. "I doubt I'm the only exception."

Titan wasn't an exception to that either, judging by the things we did together the other night. She told me she would think about what I asked. I was still waiting to hear her answer. She was going to say yes. We both knew it. But I didn't know how long she was going to drag out her decision.

But she could take all the time she needed. I wasn't going anywhere.

"Seeing anyone?" he asked.

He always asked me that, probably because we were family. "Here and there. You?"

"Here and there," he replied. "A lot of beautiful women in the world. But not a lot of remarkable ones."

Titan was the only one I'd ever met.

Our food arrived, and we discussed business, the one topic we both had a vested interest in. We could talk for hours about potential investments, Wall Street, and the stock market. When we finished lunch, I paid the tab, and Brett excused himself to the restroom. I sat at the table alone and pulled out my phone, searching through my pile of emails I had to get through.

"Diesel Hunt." A man slipped into the chair across from me.

I set down my phone and looked into the eyes of Thorn Cutler. Bright blue and narrowed, he looked just as intimidating up close as he did across the room —with his arm wrapped around Titan. I met his gaze with no surprise, rivaling his intimidation with my own confidence. "Thorn Cutler."

He leaned forward over the table, his hands together next to Brett's abandoned drink. "We haven't formally met."

"Nice to meet you." I couldn't keep the coldness out of my voice. I didn't like Titan being so close to a man that was clearly attractive and successful. He cast a shadow of ownership over her. I could even see it now—without her in the room.

"She's still thinking about your offer."

So she really told him everything. "What do you think her answer will be?"

"Yes, of course. She just needs some time to accept the specific requirements of your relationship. But I knew she would cave. She's got the hots for you…don't tell her I said that." He winked.

None of this was making sense. He obviously approved of my relationship with Titan, but he seemed to have his own form of affection for her. "What is your relationship with her?"

"I'm her friend, of course."

That was a bullshit answer. I knew it—and he knew I knew it. "Then why do I always see you two together—with your hand on her waist?"

He shrugged. "We're affectionate, I suppose."

I didn't know whether I should like him or hate him. He obviously wasn't getting in the way of me being with Titan, but it bothered me that I didn't understand his connection to her. The media portrayed them as being together—something neither one of them would confirm or deny.

Thorn adjusted his watch as he looked at me. "I'm not fucking her, if that's what you're worried about. She's all yours."

It didn't seem that way.

"I should go. I have a lunch meeting." He snatched a piece of bread from the basket and stood up. "But it was nice seeing you, Diesel Hunt." He patted my shoulder before he walked off.

I remained in my chair as I pondered the conversation I'd just had, unsure what we even talked about.

———

WHEN A WEEK PASSED and I didn't hear from her, I called her.

I was sitting in my living room with the game on the TV. I muted the sound and sat back into the couch, sitting in just my sweatpants. The phone was pressed to my ear, and I listened to it ring endlessly.

She answered with a voice that was sexy enough for me to beat off to. "Evening, Hunt."

I paused before I responded, treasuring the sound of my name on her lips. Every time she said it, it was the sexiest thing I'd ever heard. No other woman had caressed my name the way she did. She took care of it, practically rubbing her tongue across it even though my name wasn't physical in nature. "Titan."

She was quiet over the line, knowing exactly why I was calling and obviously having nothing to say about it. "Where are you?"

"In my living room."

"What are you wearing?"

I grinned. "Gray sweatpants."

"Mmm…"

I closed my eyes at the sound. I couldn't even speak to her for two minutes without being turned on. I'd spent the week beating off to our last hookup. I wasn't the kind of guy who jerked off often. I preferred sex with a real woman opposed to my hand.

But for the past week, I was beating off every morning and every night. "I miss you."

Her response was immediate even though I assumed I wouldn't get a response at all. "I miss you too."

"Then accept my offer."

"I'm still thinking about it…"

"Let me come over while you think about it." I was horny, and so was she. I could tell just by the way she breathed through the phone. If we weren't going to solve anything tonight, we might as well enjoy each other. "I'm tired of my hand. I want you."

She took another deep breath, obviously aroused by the comment. "You haven't been spending time with your girls?"

"No. You're the only one I want."

Another breath.

Even though I didn't understand what Thorn meant to her, I knew she wasn't sleeping with him. "And I'm the only man you want."

"True," she whispered. "Do you think about me when you jerk off?"

I wasn't ashamed of my answer. "Always."

"And what do you think about exactly?"

My cock hardened in my boxers. "Your tongue on my balls."

"I thought you liked that…"

"Liked it?" I whispered. "No, I fucking loved it."

Titan breathed into the phone, growing quiet.

"Just say yes, Titan. We can keep dancing around this, but we both know what's going to happen."

"What's going to happen?" she challenged.

"You're going to say yes."

"You sound certain."

"My cock is rock-hard just from listening to you. If your answer isn't yes, I'll make it a yes."

Titan released a moan so quiet I could barely hear it. "I'll be there in ten minutes."

Yes. "It's nine o'clock. I'll come to you."

"No."

"It's not safe for a beautiful woman to be out in the city right now." It was stupid to feel protective of her when she wasn't even my woman. But the compulsion was natural for me. The entire time she was on that racetrack, my heart wouldn't slow down. I was terrified she would lose control of the wheel and crash. When I'd threatened Charles Brown, I'd let my temper get the best of me, but I couldn't help myself.

"You're right, it's not safe," she said. "But I own this city. And I own everyone in it."

VICTORIA QUINN

———

THE ELEVATOR DOORS OPENED, and she stepped into my penthouse. The layout of the place was different from hers, but the spacious feel was exactly the same. The elevator opened right into my living room, and it did the same in her place.

She was in a long jacket and heels.

I could only imagine what was underneath.

I'd already poured her a drink, with a cherry and an orange peel, but the moment I saw her, I didn't care about offering it to her. I walked up to her and cupped her cheeks with both hands before I kissed her.

And I kissed her hard.

My tongue immediately went in for the kill by slipping into her mouth and finding hers. They swirled together, and I gripped her waist, breathing into her mouth at the same time. My body was out of control, desperate for the woman who had become my biggest fantasy.

She moaned right in the beginning, her hands exploring my bare chest.

I wanted to talk about our arrangement, but I was too aroused to care about that right now.

Fuck first, talk later.

We maneuvered into my bedroom, clothes hitting the floor along the way, and made it to the bed when we were both naked. I snatched a condom out of the drawer and rolled it on before I pinned myself on top of her, folding her up so I had the best position to fuck her pussy as deep as possible.

She grabbed my hips and yanked me inside her, gasping for air when she felt my big dick stretch her wide apart. "God, yes." She hooked her arms behind my shoulders, her legs wide and my arms pinned behind her knees, and moved with me every time I thrust into her.

Neither one of us cared about domination. Now, all we wanted was to get off, to fuck each other until we could think clearly again. I hadn't felt this kind of passion in years, maybe ever. My body needed her like an addict needed a drug. She was my weakness, the weakness that made me feel strong.

I fucked her hard on my bed, smashing the headboard into the wall and causing enough noise that my neighbors were bound to hear it. My mouth couldn't kiss her because I was moving too fast, thrusting too hard. I needed to breathe, to sweat, to feel.

She came immediately, in record-breaking time.

And I came to the sound of my name on her lips.

Hunt.

I filled the end of the condom, wishing it was her bare pussy instead. I'd never wanted to come inside a woman like I did with Titan. When I imagined it with other women, it was always with uncertainty. But giving Titan my desire, giving her the seed my body produced for her, sounded like the sexiest thing in the world.

I kissed her when I was finished, my cock softening inside her. I pulled out of her, watching her wince slightly once she was empty of my mass. I walked into the bathroom, cleaned off, and started the shower. Knowing her, she was probably making an attempt to get dressed and leave. She was always a flight risk—and a pain in the ass.

I rounded the corner and saw her standing naked in my bedroom. "Get in here." I gave her a look that said I wasn't going to ask her again. There was a good chance she would call my bluff, but I risked it anyway. I stepped into my large shower and let the warm water soak me to the bone.

When minutes passed, I assumed she wasn't coming.

But then she joined me. Her hair was pulled into a bun so she could keep it dry, and she stepped under the hot water with me, her beautiful body immediately soaked with the spray. Rivulets formed and dripped down her body, leading to the drain in between us.

I'd just slept with her, but I still wanted more of her. My arms wrapped around her waist, and I kissed her, giving her a soft embrace that was different from the one I'd greeted her with. My hands explored her body, feeling her firm tits and her toned tummy. I came in here to clean off, but it looked like I was about to get dirty again.

She was the one to break apart first. She grabbed my bar of body soap and then rubbed it into my chest, cleaning me off with delicate fingers. I'd never seen her treat anything so lovingly, and it made me feel like someone she actually cared about.

I watched her rub me, her red fingernails trailing over my skin. "Are you giving me a yes?"

She faltered for a moment before she continued rubbing the soap into my skin. "I'm not sure."

"Titan." I was tired of being patient with this woman. I wanted to have incredible sex with her every single day of my life. I was already in a monogamous relationship without actually being in the relationship. So far, I wasn't a big fan of it.

"You're frustrated." She looked up through her eyelashes.

"Very."

"In my defense, you wouldn't be frustrated if you just accepted my terms."

"And you wouldn't be frustrated if you accepted my terms." This could go both ways, and she knew it.

She used the bar of soap on herself, rubbing it across her stomach and her arms. "I guess we could discuss the specifics…might hit some speed bumps there."

"Such as?"

"Are you willing to get tested?"

"For STDs?" Now she was back to business, the sexy talk over.

"Yes."

"Of course. And you?"

"Yes. I don't want to use condoms anymore. Is that acceptable to you?"

If we were sitting in an office, we'd both be dressed in suits and taking notes. There'd be a lawyer on either side of the table with us. "Are you on birth control?"

"I have an IUD. It's good for another five years."

I'd never had sex without a condom before. My promiscuity never allowed me to have anything more intimate. Besides, there were lots of women who would love to be knocked up by me, to be legally bound to me forever even if I didn't love them. I could never trust a woman not to trick me. But Titan was obviously different from the rest. "Then yes."

"I'm not saying I'm agreeing to anything…but I'm curious. How long should this arrangement last?"

"As long as we want."

"We need a timetable."

"Why?" We should enjoy each other until the flame went out, whether that was in a week or in three months.

"Because we're switching. Each of us should have equal time. And I'm going first…" She stared at me like she expected me to challenge her.

Since this was her idea in the first place, I'd let her have her way. Besides, I always saved the best for last.

"So, two weeks each?"

There was no way in hell I was going to be done in two weeks. "Two months."

"Two months?" she asked incredulously. "That's a long time…one month."

"Six weeks."

Her eyes shifted back and forth as she looked into mine. "Six weeks, it is."

I was going to do whatever I wanted to her for six weeks. Tatum Titan was mine to enjoy—exclusively. I was a very lucky man.

"There are no safe words. That's the kind of trust I like to have with my partners...when there's no turning back. If you walk away, which you're allowed to do, there's no coming back. Because that trust is broken."

I couldn't picture her being into anything extreme, but if she was, I could handle it. She could whip me until I bled. It would all be worth it to have complete ownership of her for six weeks. I could do whatever I wanted with her. I could tell her to do anything, and she would obey. I already had ideas in my head. "That's fine with me—but that goes both ways."

When her eyes lost their usual callousness, I knew I hit a nerve. She wore a different look on her face, one full of uncertainty. "I...I don't know—"

"If there's anything you're unwilling to do, just tell me, and I'll steer clear." Everyone had their hard limits, stuff they weren't into.

"I'll have to think about it. You don't have any limits?"

"No." There was nothing this woman could do to me that I couldn't handle.

"Well, if you don't have any, then I can't have any. It has to be equal."

Becoming a dictator over Tatum Titan sounded

like the greatest thing in the world. I could have her whenever I wanted her. I could order her to my office and fuck her on my desk in the middle of the day. "That's fine with me."

"No one can know about our relationship besides the two of us."

"Thorn knows everything."

Her eyebrows rose to her forehead. "How did you know that?"

I felt obligated to keep the details secret, although I didn't owe him anything. "He told me."

"When did he talk to you?"

"We ran into each other at the charity gala. He didn't say anything specific…but he made it obvious that he knew we were seeing each other. So if he knows, why can't I tell my friends?"

"Because I don't trust them."

"And why should I trust your friends?"

"Because I'm the one who needs this to be a secret. If the world knew you were fucking me, it would just make you look better, make you look like the conqueror who took down the ice queen."

We lived in a world where women were held to a double standard. The more women I fucked, the more desirable I was. The fewer men Titan was with, the classier she was. It was completely unfair. "What if people think we're just dating? There's nothing wrong with that. The world doesn't need to know about our arrangement."

"They think I'm dating Thorn."

"And why don't you correct them?" I challenged.

She broke eye contact and rinsed the soap off her body.

Why wouldn't she answer me? "Are you dating him?"

"No."

"Then why do you act like it?"

"I don't act like it," she said calmly. "People see us together and think we're an item. I can't control what the media thinks."

"If you stopped attending parties together as a couple, that would probably help," I snapped.

She flashed her irritated eyes on me. "I don't want anyone to know about us, Hunt. That's the end of the discussion."

"The end of the discussion?" My teeth ground together, irritated by this stubborn woman. "I have a bit of a streak as a manwhore, alright? If I stop going out with my guys, they're gonna know something is up. I may as well just tell them."

"No way."

"They won't say anything to anyone if I ask them not to."

"I don't know them," she said. "I don't trust them."

"They're good guys, I swear."

"Good guys that sleep with my friends once and then ignore them?" she asked incredulously. "Who ghost them when they call?"

I couldn't speak to that. "Yes, they're playboys. But that doesn't mean they aren't loyal to me. If I asked them to stay quiet about it, they would."

"No."

"You need—"

"I said no."

Now my entire body tensed in anger. I looked at this beautiful woman and wanted to strangle her instead of kiss her. That was a first. "Don't fucking interrupt me." I crowded her in the shower, sticking my face close to hers in a naturally defensive state.

When she stepped back slightly, I knew she felt my rage.

"Do you understand me?" I spoke quietly, but my voice was still louder than the falling water.

She gave a slight nod.

"No. I want to hear you."

Now she narrowed her eyes in anger. "Don't push

it, Hunt." She shut off the water and got out of the shower. There was only one towel hanging on the rack, and she snatched it before she walked back into my bedroom.

We'd officially had our first fight.

I just hoped it wouldn't be our last.

FIFTEEN

Tatum

THE MORE I LOST CONTROL OF THE SITUATION, THE angrier I became.

I was used to making the rules, calling the shots, being in charge.

Then Hunt walked in and screwed everything up.

I wanted to make demands that were met. I wanted to ask for things without being questioned. But Hunt had his own requests, and most of them, if not all, were contrary to mine.

Such a pain.

I stormed out of his apartment, not because I was angry at him, but because I was frustrated with the situation. I missed the way my arrangements used to be, when I found a man I wanted and he agreed to all of my terms. Sometimes they asked for one or two exceptions, but they were always small.

Hunt wanted to flip everything upside down.

If I didn't want him so much, dream about him every night, I would abandon this attempt and move on to someone else.

But damn, I wanted this man.

I wanted him more than I'd ever wanted anyone else. Everything about him was pure sex. He was so strong, masculine, and unbelievable in bed. His strength and domination were both reasons I was attracted to him in the first place. It was pretty naïve of me to be frustrated when he retained those qualities even in our circumstances.

I went through the week, stuck in meeting after meeting. Paperwork piled up, and my four assistants couldn't even keep up. I was invited to a fashion show this week in Manhattan, the biggest one they held in America. Pilar was hitting the runway, so of course, I had to be there to support her. Not to mention, I loved the clothes.

Just like my cars, it was another weakness.

My closet was stuffed with outfits from the best designers in the world. Sometimes they were sent to me as a gift, a quiet sponsorship. Connor Suede, in particular, liked high-powered women in his clothes. And since I was one of the most influential women in the world, I got outfits before they even hit the market.

Just as I was thinking about what I was going to wear, Jessica walked inside my office with a large box. Suede's label was printed on the side, and a black bow sat secured right on top. "This was just delivered." She set it on my desk and walked away.

The second she was gone, I couldn't hold myself back. I yanked on the ribbon and opened the lid.

A note was placed inside.

TITAN,

The most beautiful dress for the most beautiful woman.

~C

THE CORNERS of my lips rose in a smile before I set the note aside and pulled out the gown. Black, slim, and elegant, it was made of soft material that stretched under my touch but never lost its elasticity. The front was a halter neck, plunging down deep with circular diamonds all along the front. The vee moved past the bust line and right to the abdomen.

It was just as beautiful as Connor claimed.

I held it up and examined it, holding my breath as I watched the pure diamonds sparkle in the light filtering through my office window. I didn't need to try it on to know it would fit me perfectly. Connor knew my exact measurements.

I returned it to the box and closed the lid before I set it off to the side. Now my mind wasn't on work, but on shoes and accessories. I'd have to hit the store before this weekend to find the perfect touches to highlight my gorgeous gown.

As an hour passed, my thoughts turned back to Hunt.

He'd probably be there.

Hitting the runway where there would be tons of beautiful woman to gawk at him sounded like his scene—along with his friends. Our last conversation ended poorly, and I knew he wouldn't contact me first. I was the one who stormed out of his apartment. The ball was in my court, and I needed to make a move.

I called his cell phone from mine and listened to it ring.

It went on for so long I assumed it would go straight to his voice mail. But he answered on the fifth ring. "Titan." His tone was sexy, but also cold. He obviously wasn't too thrilled about the way we'd left things. "Was wondering when I would hear from you."

"What made you so certain you would hear from me at all?"

I could actually hear his smile over the phone. "Just a hunch."

So arrogant. But so sexy.

"What can I do for you, Titan?"

He knew exactly why I was calling. "Wanted you to know that my outburst last week doesn't change my interest in our arrangement."

"I figured. You don't want to walk away from me as much as I don't want to walk away from you."

I didn't have as much power as I used to because he holding half of it. I was making exceptions for him, something I never did for anyone else, so he knew he was valuable. He could push and pull me much harder than the average person.

"And I'm not the kind of man who lets my woman slip away."

"I'm not your woman."

He chuckled. "Not yet."

The hairs on my arms stood on end, the goose bumps trailing all over my body.

"But you will be—very soon."

I crossed my legs under my desk, feeling my body clench for him. My thighs were so toned they were practically made of steel now. "This hasn't been easy for me. There's so many things I don't like...but I can't walk away."

Hunt stayed quiet over the line, but his smile seemed to drop. I no longer felt his confidence over the phone like I could a minute ago.

"I'm not used to negotiating. I've never been very good at it."

"I can tell."

I rolled my eyes.

He chuckled, like he knew exactly what I just did. "Why are you like this?"

I felt my heavy pen between my fingertips and tapped it against my desk pad. My computer screen had turned black from inactivity, and I could see my assistants answering phone calls from their desks. "Doesn't matter."

"Matters to me."

Swapping personal stories was something I didn't do. "Are you going to the fashion show on Saturday?"

"You can change the subject for now, but we'll revisit this conversation soon."

Not surprised.

"Yes, I'm going. I'm assuming you are as well?"

"Yes."

"Are you taking Thorn?" A hint of jealousy was in his tone. It was misplaced because it was unnecessary.

"No. He'll be in Chicago that weekend."

"So you're going alone?"

"Yes."

"I am too. But I know we won't be going home alone."

I missed that self-assured mouth all over my body. I missed the way his husky voice spoke into my ear when he was buried inside me. I found myself tossing and turning in the middle of the night, covered in sweat as I thought about this man.

"Let's continue this conversation then—and finish it."

———

MY DRIVER DROPPED me off at the entrance, and the second I stepped out, photographers flashed their cameras. I heard someone say, "Where's Thorn Cutler? What went wrong?" I ignored the idiotic question and walked forward. Like the good specimen I was, I posed for a few photos before I walked inside.

People were gathered together near the bar, getting their drinks in their finest wear. All the men were in suits and tuxes, with the exception of a few designers. The women were in cocktail dresses like I was, wearing the designers they loved the most. I held my silver clutch at my side and moved through the crowd, greeting familiar faces and making small talk.

I stopped when I saw a familiar face, a face that came to me every night in my dreams.

Diesel Hunt.

With Pine and Mike next to him, he stood with both of his hands in his pockets. A beautiful blonde was beside him in a silver gown. Her hand was tucked into his arm, holding on to him like he was her date for the evening.

I felt a jolt of jealousy.

But then I let it pass, dissolve into the air. I brushed it off like it was nothing, knowing Hunt's personal life was none of my business. Until we signed the paperwork, he wasn't mine to think about. And even when he was mine, he wasn't mine to own. There was no love between us. We'd be lucky to have friendship.

I didn't care.

"Titan." Connor's deep voice came from behind me.

I smiled before I turned around, coming face-to-face with the handsome blond who made the most beautiful clothes in the world.

He had an Old Fashioned for me, remembering what I liked to drink. "You look beautiful." He handed me the glass before he leaned in and kissed me on the cheek.

"Thank you. You look very handsome yourself."

When he pulled away, he was still close to me. Only a few inches separated us, and I could smell the mixture of mint and bourbon on his breath. In a gray suit with a black collared shirt and black tie, he looked muscular beneath his clothing. As one of the tallest men in the world, he stood out. Even though he had pretty eyes and a fair face, it didn't lighten his dark appearance. He emitted a dark aura that all women picked up on. The instant I was the recipient of that gaze, I couldn't turn away. "Don't tell anyone I said this…" His hand moved around my waist, and he pulled me close to him, touching me like a man touched his woman. "But you make that dress look better than anything my ladies are gonna show on the runway."

"You flatter me, Connor."

"It's honest flattery." He pulled away but took longer to remove his hand from my waist. "I'm glad you're here."

"I wouldn't miss it. I need a reason to wear this beautiful dress. I wore it around the house all day—but no one got to see it."

"I'm glad I got to see it." His eyes moved all the way down my body, settling on the deep slit right between my breasts. It wasn't the first time he'd looked at me like that. He'd looked at me that way a few times—in bed.

"It was nice to see you, Connor. I'll let you get back to work."

"Will do. But let's meet up afterward." He kissed me on the cheek before he walked away.

The second he was gone, I had a new visitor.

Hunt didn't speak a word when he came to my side. He stood there as a presence, a hostile ball of energy that absorbed the air around him. He looked at me with a deadly expression, the kind of look an executioner gave before he chopped off a criminal's head.

Except I wasn't a criminal. "Hunt." I extended my hand to shake his.

He didn't look at it, dismissing my advance.

My stare hardened. "When an associate offers to shake your hand, you do it." No one was watching us, but that didn't matter. If he couldn't keep up this pretense now, how would he manage later?

Hunt shook my hand. "You and Connor are close." It wasn't a question, but it certainly sounded like it—full of accusation as well.

"I love his pieces. This dress is his."

His eyes roamed down my body, paying special attention to the same slit Connor had been staring at just a moment ago. "He dressed you well—like he knows your body."

"It is his living, Hunt." My eyes drifted to the blond woman still standing with his friends. Her eyes were glued to Hunt's back, counting down the seconds before he returned to her. "Your date seems lonely."

"She's not my date." He returned his hands to the pockets of his slacks. His shoulders looked appetizing in the slim-fit suit he wore. He'd shaved before arriving tonight, and his jaw was so smooth I wanted to rub my fingers across the skin just so I could feel it. I wanted to press kisses there, exploring his masculine jaw for as long as I wanted. My attraction to Hunt was so passionate that it made my body feel more alive than it ever had before. I was turning my world upside down for him—but I knew it would be worth it.

"I don't think she knows that."

"She will very soon." His brown eyes were glued to mine, ignoring everyone else in the room except me. He hardly blinked, staring at me with an intensity that would make a lesser woman look away.

But I never looked away.

"You have no idea how hard it is to stand here and not kiss you."

My chest froze in place as I stopped breathing for a few seconds. My entire body shut down, but when it turned back on, I was burning at a higher intensity than before. I wanted to hook one leg around his waist and grind against him like I had on his yacht last month. I wanted to enjoy him in bed, smothering the sheets with his smell mixed with mine. I wanted to lick the sweat off his chest when he finished fucking me the way I liked. "You have no idea how hard it is not to fuck you right now."

"If you made a move, I wouldn't stop you." He inched closer to me, keeping his hands in his pockets to project the aura that our conversation was purely friendly, not a battle of restrained passion.

"Good thing I'm patient." I spotted the blond woman glide toward him, making her move to catch him before he slipped away for good. "It was nice to see you, Hunt." I said the words as she walked up. "Have a good evening." I drifted away so I wouldn't have to introduce myself to her. I wasn't going to be polite to a woman who wanted to sleep with the same man I was obsessed with.

Hunt caught up to me, his hand moving to my elbow. He came up behind me and spoke into my ear, keeping his voice low so no one could hear us. "Even before we come to an agreement, I'm yours. Understand me?"

Hearing him give himself to me made me want to ditch the party and head straight home. "Yes."

Now his lips were so close they brushed against the shell of my ear. "And you're mine?"

I knew he was referring to Connor, who greeted me like we had a history that was more passionate than a mere business relationship.

"Tell me you're mine." His hand gripped me tighter. "Or I'll make you mine right now."

I turned my face his way, my lips almost coming into contact with his. "You already know you're the only man I'm going home with."

———

AFTER THE SHOW, everyone broke apart and hit the various bars around the building. Appetizers were passed around, and Connor Suede was bombarded by compliments from people in the industry and even people he didn't know. Sometimes his eyes landed on mine across the room. He was searching for me, either interested in me or the gown he designed for me to wear tonight.

"Ms. Titan." Brett Maxwell walked up to me with a drink in his hand. "You're my favorite person to bump into." He shook my hand before he leaned in and kissed me on the cheek. The area around his mouth had a slight line of hair, and it rubbed against my skin before he pulled away.

"You're my favorite person too—because you know everything about cars."

He smiled at the compliment. "And you know how to drive them. You hit the racetrack pretty hard."

"I just wanted to test my girl on the asphalt."

"I hope she impressed you."

"She definitely did."

He smiled before he tapped his glass against mine. "I'll drink to that." He brought the glass to his lips.

I did the same, emptying my glass and feeling the burn down my throat. I was on my third Old Fashioned, and I needed to cut myself off. I wasn't even buzzed because I had a high tolerance for alcohol, but I still didn't want to overdo it, not when I was going to meet up with Hunt later.

He eyed my empty glass, obviously thinking about how quickly I drank the whole thing, but he was a gentleman and didn't say anything about it. "I was going to wait until Monday to mention this, but since I have you here now, I want to run something by you."

"Shoot."

"I want to shoot a commercial for my Bullet model—and I was wondering if you'd be in it."

"Me?" I asked in surprise. "Really?"

"Are you kidding? The richest woman in the world driving my car down the Amalfi coastline? The wind in her hair? Shades on her face? It would be great. It appeals to every demographic, to women who want a true luxury car, and to men who would love to attract a woman just like you."

People gave me a lot of compliments, but not all of them were genuine. They said things I wanted to hear just to get something out of me. But I'd never cared for flattery or validation. I preferred to keep company with those who challenged me, who would tell me the truth as they saw it. But Brett seemed genuine. He was endearing and not just because he was extremely handsome. He'd always been respectful toward me, treating me as an equal with an extra touch of admiration. I wished more men could be like him, not feel threatened by my success or my mind, but to appreciate it. "That sounds like a lot of fun, Brett."

"Does that mean you're in?"

"I think so."

He grinned, showing all of his perfectly straight teeth. "That's awesome. Diesel Hunt is also on board. I thought I could have the two of you racing down the coastline, cutting each other off as you sprint to the finish line."

I didn't know Hunt was going to be a part of this. But if Brett had told me that beforehand, it wouldn't have changed my answer. However, a warning would have been nice. I didn't want to be seen spending too much time with Hunt. "That sounds great."

"Originally, I wanted you two to be in the same car, like a couple. Sex sells, and what would be hotter than two executives enjoying the sunset in one of my cars? But Hunt didn't go for it."

And I knew why. Perhaps he understood me

better than I gave him credit for. "Leave a message with my office, and we'll set something up."

"Sounds like a plan."

A tall woman came to his side, sliding her arm around his waist and placing her palm on his chest. I recognized her from the runway, one of the models who'd shown off Connor's new line of gowns. She had dark skin, plump lips, and legs that went on for days. She whispered something to him in French, her lips near his ear.

He hugged her into his body and said something back. "Excuse me, Titan. Have a good night."

"You too." I watched him walk off with his date, the tall woman still shorter than him in her heels. She pressed against him like she didn't want to be in the public eye for a moment longer, but on her back on his sheets.

Watching the way he gripped her waist as they walked away reminded me of the way Hunt gripped me. There were more similarities between the two men, other features I couldn't put my finger on. But I knew there was a connection between them—a big one.

———

I SAT in the back seat of my car, my driver taking me back to my penthouse a few blocks away. I'd stayed out with Isa and Pilar until one in the morning. I wasn't tired just yet, but if I stayed out too long, I wouldn't be able to say two words to Hunt.

But he hadn't called me yet.

I kept thinking about that blond supermodel on his arm, the way she looked at him like she owned him.

Bitch, please.

Hunt made it clear he wasn't going to fuck her tonight, and he made sure I wasn't going to be with Connor either. That was all the reassurance I needed. Neither one of us was interested in other people right now—just each other.

But I wasn't just interested—I was obsessed.

My phone rang, and Hunt's name appeared on my screen.

I hit the button on the ceiling and closed the shade between Lucas and me before I answered. "Thought you'd be too tired by now."

"I'm never too tired for you."

The inside of my mouth moistened at the sound of his voice. I could spend all night just running my tongue along his body, tasting his delicious flesh. I didn't need to sleep with him to feel satisfied. Just sucking that big cock was enough for me. "How's your girl?"

"You tell me," he said. "Since you're my girl."

I smiled automatically since no one was around to witness it. He was a smooth talker, and he was so good with the lines he actually impressed me. And I wasn't an easy woman to impress.

"Where are you?"

"My driver is taking me home."

"Then I'll meet you over there." He waited for my objection.

But I certainly didn't have one.

"There better not be too much talking. Watching you walk around in that dress all night tested my patience. I might rip it when I take it off you."

"Then why don't we skip the talking and get straight to business?"

A long pause ensued. "I like the way you do business, Titan."

———

I GOT on my knees in my panties as he sat on the couch, his shirt unbuttoned and his slacks at his knees.

I grabbed his hands and positioned them on the

cushion, his palms facing the ceiling. "Don't move." I met his look with a stern one, telling him I meant business. I wasn't the kind of woman who settled for less than what I deserved.

He kept his hands still, but his eyes narrowed on my face.

I craned my neck down and brought his enormous cock into my mouth.

The second my tongue touched his tip, he leaned back and released a long moan.

I worked his dick with my mouth, moving all the way down and then back up again. I moved slowly, dragging my tongue along his throbbing vein.

"Titan…"

I loved hearing him say my name. Pleasing him was almost better than pleasing myself—almost. I tasted the lubrication that came from his tip, loving how delicious it was in my mouth. He tasted like a man, a mega dose of masculinity.

His hand slid across his thigh and into my hair, where he got a fistful of the strands.

I yanked his wrist down then slapped him across the face. "I said don't move."

His cheek didn't turn red because I didn't hit him hard enough. He stilled at the shock of the impact, but instead of looking angry, he closed his eyes and clenched his jaw, his chest rising with the deep breath he took.

I worked his cock again, noticing how much harder he was in my mouth.

I knew he would like leaving me in charge.

I worked his dick until he was soaked in my saliva, slippery and warm. I pulled his enormous dick out of my mouth and then positioned myself in front of him, cupping my tits around his length so they squeezed him on both sides.

Hunt looked down at what I was doing and sucked in a breath between his teeth. His hands balled into fists on the cushions, and his jaw clenched all over again.

I moved my wet tits up and down his length then kissed his masculine mouth.

He barely kissed me back, his breathing deep and rugged. After a moment of gaining his ground, he kissed me back, his tongue moving into my mouth and greeting mine sensually.

His hands weren't on my body, but I felt my nerves firing off. I felt the moisture between my legs pooling in my panties. My thighs were shaking, and my lungs ached every time I breathed. I wanted to ride his cock now, but I wanted to do this too. His thick cock pushed through the valley of my tits over and over, sliding along the soft skin until I moved up then pushed him through again.

He moaned into my mouth, his warm breath filling my lungs.

I moaned in response, our mutual arousal taking me to new heights.

His hands palmed my tits and squeezed them harder against his dick, giving himself more friction as he thrust upward.

I pushed his hands down then slapped him harder than I had the first time.

He clenched his jaw and sucked in a breath. "Fuck, woman. You're just turning me on more."

I grabbed my tits and worked his length again. "You can touch me when I say you can."

He moaned. "I want to touch you now. Fuck, let me touch you."

"No." I spoke against his mouth, our breaths falling on each other. His cock rubbed against my voluptuous skin.

He thrust his hips upward, moving with me as he kissed me. His breathing grew deeper and deeper, turning shaky and heated. He looked more like a man when he was on the verge of exploding, about to give me all the come that had built deep inside his balls. "I'm gonna come all over your tits."

"Not yet."

He growled then bit my bottom lip, nibbling on it harshly.

I bit him back, showing the same ferocity.

"You're killing me…"

I moved harder and faster, torturing him on purpose.

His hands formed fists again, and he panted. The veins in his neck were strained because he was tightening his jaw so much. He ground his teeth together, the noise nearly audible. "You want to come, Hunt?"

He stared me down, his powerful chest rising and falling deeply.

"Tell me."

He locked his eyes on mine, his lips no longer kissing me. "Yes."

"You want to come on my tits?"

"Fuck yes."

"What about my face?"

His eyes darkened in a way I'd never seen them before. He looked like he hated me but wanted to fuck me even more because of it. "I'd love to come on your face…"

"Then you officially have my permission." I grabbed his large hands and placed them on either side of my breasts.

The second his fingertips touched the bare skin of my tits, he squeezed them harshly then guided me up and down, moving me faster than I was going before. He thrust upward at the same time, and within ten seconds, he came.

All over me.

He came on my chin, my neck, and all over my tits.

"Fuck…" With every pump he gave, he squirted more all over me. Drops of come were everywhere, rubbing into my skin as his dick still moved. It was smeared all over my flesh, the scent of his come heavy in my nostrils.

He admired his handiwork, seeing the white globs of his essence all over the place. His cock softened between my tits, but he still rubbed his own seed onto himself, sliding through the stickiness. "I've never fucked such a nice pair of tits."

"And such a nice dick has never fucked my tits before." I wiped my fingers across my chest before I stuck them in my mouth, sucking his come from the tips.

"My fucking god." He squeezed my tits harshly, his body reacting in the only way it could —instinctively.

"We aren't done yet." I rose to my feet and pulled my panties down my legs. A line of lubrication formed between the lace and my pussy as I pulled the fabric down. It finally broke apart, but the tops of my inner thighs were wet with my own lubrication. Hunt made me wetter and wetter every time.

Hunt stared at the area between my legs, that masculine intensity coming into his eyes. He just finished an orgasm that I made him work for, but he seemed aroused again. His dick was semihard, but it wouldn't take long until it was full mast.

I took a seat beside him then snapped my fingers. "On your knees."

He stared at me coldly, like he wasn't going to cooperate even if I asked him again.

"Now."

After seconds of eye contact, he moved to the floor and positioned himself between my legs. He spread my legs far apart and settled his face against my slick folds. "I'm not here because you asked. I'm here because there's nothing I want more than to eat your pussy for the rest of the night—and make you come as many times as you want."

———

IT WAS three in the morning.

We lay on the couch together, his arm cocooning me into his chest. His chin rested on my head, and we both smelled like a mixture of sex, perfume, and cologne. We were both naked, but the heat generated by his body kept us warm. My bedroom was just down the hallway, but neither one of us moved.

His hand slowly slid through my hair, caressing the strands down to my shoulder. "So, are we going to talk about the final details?"

I didn't need much sleep, but after the long night I'd had, I was too tired for a coherent conversation. "Tomorrow."

"It is tomorrow."

"You know what I mean."

"How about we go out to dinner? If we're in a public place, we'll do more talking than fucking."

That was too risky. "I don't want anyone to overhear us."

"My place or yours, then?"

"Mine."

"Alright. What time?"

"Five."

"And in the meantime…" He nuzzled his face against mine and closed his eyes.

He wasn't sleeping over. That was a stipulation we

had yet to discuss. "Brett Maxwell mentioned his commercial idea."

"Are you interested?"

"I love his cars and I love Italy, so naturally, yes."

"Even though I'll be in the commercial too?"

"As long as I win the race."

He smiled against my hairline. "Everything is always a competition with you."

"Life is a competition."

"Not always," he whispered. "Should we meet with him and discuss the details? It's the perfect time of year to head over there."

"I've got a lot of stuff going on, but I could move some things around to accommodate the trip."

"As can I." His fingers continued to stroke my hair.

When I thought about Brett Maxwell, the question that had been sitting in the back of my mind came to the forefront. "You're related to him, aren't you?"

He smiled again. "Picked up on that, huh?"

"Is he your cousin?"

"No. My brother."

They didn't have the same last name, so I'd immediately dismissed that theory. But when I looked at their such similar appearance, I knew it was true.

They had the same eyes, same facial structure, the same everything. "Why is his last name different from yours?"

"Because we're half-brothers. My mother was married before she met my father."

"Oh…" I never knew that.

"Her first husband died in a car crash. Then she met my father. Brett was pretty young at the time. He and I are only a few years apart."

"You seem close."

"We are. Blood can do that to people."

"Why aren't you more forthcoming about that connection?" Hunt could have mentioned it several times, but he never did. He purposely kept me, as well as the rest of the world, in the dark.

"Brett doesn't like to be associated with the Hunt bloodline. He and my father never got along. When my mother passed away, my father had to raise us. Brett had nowhere else to go, so he stuck around, but my father treated him like dirt every single day." His breathing changed, and he tensed underneath me, obviously thinking about a past he'd rather forget.

I felt terrible for asking to begin with. I didn't want him to pry into my past, so I should quiet my curiosity. "Both of you are very charming. I've always liked Brett. He treats me like a person, not just a woman. He's very secure with his own success and isn't intimidated by mine. A real man isn't intimidated by anyone."

"He gets that from me."

I rolled my eyes. "You probably get it from him, actually."

"We get a lot of great traits from each other. He gives me shit when I'm being a dumbass, and I pick on him when he's being a douche. It's what brothers do."

"Sibling love."

"You don't have any brothers or sisters, right?"

Only child. "Nope." I changed the subject before he could venture down that road any further. "It's getting late… I should get to bed." I got off his body and pulled on my panties. My dress was in a pile on the floor, but I was too tired to pick it up. My heels had been kicked off along the way, scattered into two different places.

Hunt got up next, a statue of pure manliness. He pulled on his boxers, sheathing his powerful, thick, and wonderful dick.

I hit the home button on my phone and checked the screen, wondering if there were any important emails I should know about. A message from Connor sat at the top. *Want to meet up?*

I hit the home button again and hid the message.

Judging from the sour look on his face, he'd already seen it. "That bed of yours is pretty big…"

I knew exactly what he was asking. Letting him sleep over didn't sound like the worst thing in the world. He was very comfortable, despite how hard and rigid his body was. And his melodic breathing acted as a lullaby. But I'd been sleeping alone for a long time, and I had no intention of changing it. "Not when you toss and turn all night."

When Hunt got my hint, he didn't press it. He pulled each piece of his suit back on, taking his time as he fastened his belt and buttoned his shirt. Now that his hair was messy, he looked even sexier than he had at the beginning of the evening.

I walked him to the elevator doors, exhausted but still wide awake because he was there. I still in just my panties, my tits hard from the cold air.

His eyes roamed over my body, his jaw slowly tightening as he looked me up and down like it was the first time he'd seen me that evening. "You expect me to leave when you look like that?"

I moved into his body and rose on my tiptoes, much shorter than I was earlier since my five-inch heels were gone. I pressed my mouth to his and gave him a soft kiss, my chest pressed against his.

He kissed me back with a quiet moan, his arms circling my body.

My fingers rubbed against his chin, feeling the shadow that had started to grow along his jaw. "You'll be seeing a lot more of it—so don't worry."

SIXTEEN

Hunt

I was just about to leave my penthouse when Brett called me.

"What's up?" I stepped into the elevator and rode it to the lobby. My cock was already battling a boner because I was on my way to Titan's, to see that beautiful creature who gave the best head in the world.

She put every other woman to shame.

I didn't realize I was capable of such climaxes, of being pleased so deeply. I didn't need to guide her to do the things I wanted. I didn't have to take the initiative. She knew exactly how to please a man.

She knew exactly how to please me.

All I cared about was getting more from this woman, not running off and finding the next substitute. Women came and went like commodities, holding no real value other than being a distraction. A few exceptional women had graced my bed, but none who compared to Tatum Titan.

She was something else.

Now my life had a new excitement, a new vigor. Ambition wasn't the only thing on my mind anymore. Now I craved a passionate kiss in front of the fire, a touch in public that was too intimate for anyone to see.

Now I only craved her.

Brett answered. "I'm surprised you're awake so early."

"It's 4:30," I said sarcastically.

"But I know you're a night owl," he teased. "I was going to see if I could get you and Titan together tonight. You know, to discuss the commercial. Time is ticking."

Why did my brother have to be a pain in the ass today? "What time?"

"About seven?"

That should be enough time for us to talk and have a good fuck. "That works for me. Let me know what she says."

"Will do."

My driver met me at the sidewalk and drove me downtown to her building. I took the elevator to her floor and stepped into her living room, seeing that it was meticulously clean—like always. It didn't seem like I'd just tit-fucked her on the couch yesterday then ate her pussy until she came three times.

She stepped out of the kitchen in jeans and a t-shirt.

I'd never seen Tatum Titan in jeans and a t-shirt.

Ever.

She was always wearing a dress or a skirt—and her stilettos. When she dressed casually, her beauty was more natural. She didn't seem so hard, so cold. But she still possessed the same aura her executive power gave her. If I'd met her for the first time right now and had no idea who she was, I would still feel her confidence and poise. "Hey."

"Hey." She set two glasses on the dining table, two Old Fashioneds. She placed each one at different ends of the table, designating where we would be sitting for our meeting. In her tight black shirt, the small of her back was noticeable as well as her incredible rack. She slowly walked toward me, barefoot as her small feet tapped against the hardwood floor. The closer she came, the more her head tilted up to look at me since I was a foot taller than she.

She rose on her tiptoes and kissed me, greeting me like she'd missed me as much as I missed her.

Even though it'd only been a day.

I loved these first kisses as much as the final kisses of the night. Something about her affection seduced me, made my chest rumble in approval. She was so sexy that it hurt sometimes. My body couldn't contain its neediness.

She pulled away before the kiss led to anything else. "Glad you're here."

"Me too."

She walked to the table and took a seat. "Would you like something else to drink?"

"This is perfect." I sat down, annoyed that there were at least six feet in between us. The floor-to-ceiling windows showed the city behind us, the sun slowly drifting behind the skyscrapers.

She organized a folder of papers before she slid it across the surface toward me—along with a pen.

I wasn't going to sign a damn thing. "Did Brett call you?"

"He did."

"And?"

"I told him we'd meet for dinner."

"Okay. So let's get this over with. I've got to have

you before we leave—otherwise, I'm not going to be able to focus."

She met my gaze with the typical sharpness in her eyes. "You won't be having me, Hunt. I'll be having you."

Fuck, she drove me wild.

"Let's begin." She drank from her glass before she licked her lips, switching into her executive mode. "For the next six weeks, you're mine exclusively. Anytime we're alone together, you're to obey me. When I ask you to do something, you do it. If you don't, you'll be punished."

If she was going to punish me by slapping me, bring it on.

"Do you understand?"

I drank from my glass. "Roger that."

"Our relationship is to remain a secret. You are not to tell anyone about us."

Our first bump in the road. "I understand why you want it that way, but that's not going to work. My buddies will know something is up."

"Then do whatever you need to do to eliminate their suspicions."

"How will I do that if I'm always with you? If they catch me in a lie, they're going to pester me until

I come clean. I may as well be up front about it so they'll keep their mouths shut."

"No." She flipped the page like the decision had already been made.

"I'm just being realistic here."

"You told me you were a gentleman." She gave me a look full of accusation. "Unless that was a lie?"

"I never lie."

"Good. That brings me to my next point." She rested her elbows on the table but kept her back straight. "Total honesty—from both of us."

"Not a problem."

"Neither is it for me." Her eyes shifted back to her paper.

"I don't tell my guys about all the women I've been with—since they're one-time things. But if I have a three-month relationship with you, a monogamous one, that's not going to be easy to hide. If your friends know about us, then mine deserve to know too."

"I'm not going to repeat myself, Hunt." That cold gaze was on me again. "I don't need to go into the specifics of why this is important to me. I have far more to lose than you do. If this is something you can't do, the offer is off the table."

Her request was a pain in the ass, but I

understood her issue. Trust was obviously something she didn't hand out freely, like candy on Halloween.

"So can you do that, Hunt?"

I wanted this woman so much I was willing to do anything to have her. "Yes."

"Great. Let's move on——"

"But I want to know what the deal is with Thorn."

Her eyes slowly moved back to me, her irises the color of impenetrable jade. "I'm not sleeping with him. That's all you need to know."

"Why are you pretending to be with him if you aren't with him?"

"I don't see how that pertains to our arrangement, so there's no need to discuss it. He's a very close friend, a business partner, and whatever the specifics of our relationship are don't concern you."

The weight of her words hit me right in the chest. "So every time we attend an event, you're going to be with him?"

"Most likely. But I wouldn't go with you anyway, so it doesn't matter."

If she wasn't sleeping with him, then it wasn't my business. But that didn't quench my curiosity. Every time I saw her touch him, it made me angry. "Have you ever slept with him?"

"My past isn't relevant to our arrangement either."

My eyes narrowed. "Is that a yes?"

"No. It's no answer at all."

"Titan." I stopped myself from clenching my jaw, afraid I was going to break it one of these days. "You're spending time with this man when you're supposed to be mine. I have a right to know."

"If you trust me, it shouldn't matter." She rested her elbows on the table and leaned forward, locking her eyes on mine. "Do you trust me, Hunt?"

Tatum Titan was a woman woven in a web of ambitions, secrets, and sex. For every wall that surrounded her, there was another one behind it. She was layered, like an onion that didn't seem to have a center. All I knew was her body, the way it reacted to mine every time I touched her. All I knew was the connection we had, the strong passion we only had for each other. That was something I knew —and enough to trust her. Without asking her, I knew she only wanted me. Whether she'd slept with Thorn or not, I was obviously the only man she wanted. I had no reason to be threatened—by anyone. "I do."

"Then we shouldn't have a problem."

"Do you trust me?" I countered.

She was quiet for so long it didn't seem like she was going to say anything. "I think so."

It was obvious she had trust issues. I should be grateful I didn't get a straight no from her.

"We shouldn't discuss business when we're together—conflict of interest."

"Our businesses have nothing to do with each other."

"I still think we should keep them separate."

"Fine." I didn't want to talk about work when I was with her anyway. All I wanted to do was talk about all the dirty things we would do together.

"You'll need to submit your test before we stop using condoms."

"That goes for you too."

She didn't object. "I should have that in a few days."

"Me too."

"I understand this probably doesn't need to be said but...there's never going to be anything more between us besides a physical relationship. Love isn't something that interests me. I can tell it doesn't interest you either, so it shouldn't be a problem."

No, there wouldn't be a problem. Women only wanted me for my money or my bed. None of them wanted me for me. I'd settled on a life of solitude a long time ago. It recently had felt lonely, but now I was rejuvenated again. "You don't want to have a family someday?"

"That's a sexist question."

"Wasn't meant to be one. I'm only curious."

"I do, actually," she said. "But I still have a few more years before I needed to worry about it. What about you?"

"Sometimes I think about it…sometimes I don't."

She didn't press me further on it. "Six weeks from today, our roles will switch. You'll be the one in charge, and I'll be the one to obey."

My chest tightened at the thought. I would love to overpower her, to completely dominate her after she dominated me. She could push me as hard as she wanted because I intended to do the same to her. I wouldn't break—so she couldn't either. "Sounds good to me."

It was the first time she'd hesitated in the conversation, looking down at the table instead of at me.

I saw the uncertainty. "It'll be alright, Titan."

Her fingertips were still painted red from the prior week. The color looked great on her, complimenting her slightly tanned skin. Not a single one was chipped because she obviously didn't bite her nails. She looked through her folder of papers before she pulled two pieces from the pile. A sigh escaped her lips.

I didn't blink as I stared at her, not wanting to miss a single thing.

"This is hard for me, Hunt. Harder than I make it seem..." She didn't show a vulnerable side to herself, ever. I wasn't even sure if this was a moment of weakness, instead just quiet reflection. "I've never accommodated a man like this. In fact, no one has ever asked so much of me before. I'm only giving it to you because...I want this to happen."

"I want it to happen too."

"I think I still need to think about it... I'm not scared of many things, but I'm scared of this."

I was the first man she was giving herself to. She was giving me her soul, letting me hold it for six weeks. "You have no reason to be scared, Titan. I'll take good care of you. And that's a promise."

She cleared her throat before she pushed the paper toward me. "The NDA."

I didn't even look at it. "I told you I wouldn't sign it."

"I'm willing to sign one too."

"I never asked." It was a stupid piece of paper, something with little legal consequence. We both had big arsenals, and we could start a world war if we wanted to—but where would that get us? "I'm not gonna change my mind about this. I live in a world of contracts. Something like this, something beautiful, is above that." I picked it up and ripped it into shreds before I left the pile on the table. "I know you feel the same way."

She considered me with a heated expression, irritated she couldn't get me to cooperate with everything she wanted. She had to keep making exceptions for me, and she questioned her strength for allowing it to happen. Whatever thoughts she had were mysterious to me, but once she picked up the paper and ripped it into pieces, I knew she'd yielded to me. "I do."

I was tired of waiting. The sooner we started, the sooner I got to have her. I wanted to officially be hers, have her officially be mine. "I'll take care of that test tomorrow. The second the results are cleared, we're going to start. No more waiting."

She stared at me with the same gaze made of steel. "No more waiting."

———

I LEFT for the restaurant ten minutes before she did, to make sure our arrivals weren't conspicuous. My brother knew me well, better than most, and he would detect something if I left too many breadcrumbs.

I took a seat at his table and ordered a glass of wine.

He greeted me with a handshake, treating me like a business associate instead of a brother when we were in public. Most people didn't know about Brett since he was older than me. People just assumed I had the one younger brother, Jax. "Get shit-faced last night?"

"No." I drank around the clock, but I didn't lose my control. I didn't like losing my mind, unable to remember a night I'd experienced. Drunk men always acted like idiots, and I certainly didn't want to be an idiot.

"Did you go home with that blonde?"

"No."

"That's too bad."

I couldn't even remember that woman's name. She was a model, but nothing in comparison to Tatum Titan. She hadn't held my interest longer than two seconds.

Brett eyed his watch. "Titan is always punctual. I'm surprised she's not here."

Because she was forced to be late—because of

me. "She'll arrive when she means to. She's important enough that she knows people will wait."

"That's an understatement," he said with a chuckle. "She looked beautiful in that dress she wore last night."

"She did." But she looked more beautiful when the dress was abandoned on the floor.

"Women like her don't come around very often. They don't have her kind of success, and even if they do, they're usually cut down by the haters. It takes a woman with a serious backbone to get to where she is now."

He praised Titan a lot, to the point where I grew suspicious.

"If she weren't with Thorn, I'd make a move."

I shouldn't feel jealous since he wasn't going to make a move, but knowing my equally handsome brother wanted to fuck my woman made me uncomfortable. I wanted to claim her as mine and tell him never to look at her like that again, but I couldn't.

Because I promised Titan I wouldn't.

I gripped my glass in my fingertips, using it as an outlet for my anger. A punch to his face would be better, but that would be a dead giveaway of my feelings for her. So I drank my drink, using the alcohol to steel my nerves.

"There she is."

She wasn't in her jeans anymore. She was in a deep blue cocktail dress, strappy heels on her feet. If someone told me she'd just been casual thirty minutes ago, I wouldn't have believed them unless I saw it with my own eyes. A silver clutch was in her hand when she arrived at the table. "Good evening, gentleman." She shook Brett's hand first. "Nice to see you again."

"Always a pleasure," Brett said, wearing an affectionate smile.

She turned to me next with a slight change in her eyes. She grabbed my hand and shook it, treating me exactly the same as she did Brett. But she definitely looked at me differently, gave me a stare that was far more intense. Just the touch of our hands affected us in intimate ways. I thought about the way she pushed her tits together and moved up and down my length. It was a thought I could never get out of my head.

We took our seats. I almost ordered an Old Fashioned for her, but I thought that would be too obvious.

We walked about the commercial, listening to Brett's vision. He and I exchanged ideas, and Titan was on board with it. We would use two cars, one in black and one in gray. They were the two most sought-after colors in the market.

"What about next week?" Brett asked. "I can make the arrangements. All expenses paid—of course."

"I can make that work," I said. "I'll take care of a few things at the office and work remotely."

"Shouldn't be a problem for me either," Titan said. "I have a meeting on Wednesday, but I should be able to reschedule it."

"Great," Brett said. "If you could both let me know by tomorrow afternoon, I'll get everything settled. I can book the plane tickets and the hotel accommodations."

"I'd like to take my own plane, if that's okay," Titan said. "You two are more than welcome to come along."

A woman with her own jet—hot. I had one of my own too, but not all wealthy people could afford such luxuries. "I'll take you up on that offer."

"I will as well," Brett said.

I hid my annoyance when I knew my brother was coming along. Fucking all the way to Italy sounded like a fun plane ride to me.

"I'll take care of the hotel arrangements," Brett

said. "If you have a preference on anything, your assistants can talk to mine, and everything will be taken care of."

"Perfect." I forced myself not to stare at Titan as hard as I normally did. My expression was easy to read, just like a picture book. Everyone in the room would know I wanted to fuck her—if I wasn't already fucking her.

"Sounds good." Titan set down a hundred-dollar bill for her portion of the meal. "I should get going. I'm meeting someone for coffee."

Was she really? And if so, who? It better not be fucking Connor Suede. I hated that prick. "Have a good evening, Titan."

"You too, Hunt." She didn't look at me as she said it, being colder to me than usual to compensate for our obvious attraction. "Good night, Brett."

"Good night, Titan." He shook her hand before she walked away.

She turned our back to us and walked out of the restaurant, her hips swaying.

Brett's eyes moved to her ass as he drank his wine.

I was supposed to bite my tongue and not give a damn. A beautiful and intelligent woman like Titan was going to be gawked at everywhere she went. She wasn't my girlfriend, so I didn't have the right to rip everyone's eyes out.

But I couldn't help it.

"Look at her ass again, and I'll choke you."

Brett's eyes drifted back to me, and he slowly lowered his wineglass. His brow furrowed in confusion, obviously unsure if I was joking.

Even though it was fucking clear that I wasn't joking.

"Excuse me?" he asked, totally perplexed.

"You heard me, asshole." I didn't flinch in my stare, telling him this was a fight he didn't want to pursue.

He shifted his weight as he looked at me, his countenance hardening just like mine. My older brother was just as stubborn as I was, if not more. If someone challenged him to a fight, he didn't back down. "You have a thing for her?"

How were Titan and I going to manage this? We hadn't even started, and it was a struggle. "No. But don't disrespect her in my presence."

"Disrespect her?" he asked incredulously. "I've done nothing but praise her—to her face and behind her back."

"Then stop staring at her ass."

"I wasn't."

"Don't lie to me. You aren't good at it."

He leaned over the table and lowered his voice. "If I were staring at her ass, I would say it. I would say it just to piss you off more than anything else. But I was looking at the blonde at the other table—the one with huge tits."

I glanced over my shoulder discreetly and saw the exact woman he was talking about. She was right in the line of sight where Brett had been looking. His story checked out. I faced him again, but I refused to admit I was wrong.

I never admitted I was wrong.

Brett tapped his fingers against the table. "Diesel."

My gaze didn't flinch.

"I'm gonna ask you again. You've got a thing for Tatum Titan?"

I didn't want to lie to my brother. I didn't lie to him about anything, and not just because he was family. He was one of the men I respected most in the world, retaining a positive attitude when he'd been treated like shit his whole life. "No." It burned me from the inside out to look him in the eye and lie. I prided myself on my honesty. I was the kind of guy who said the shit you didn't want to hear. I was honest to a fault.

"Then what's the deal?"

"I respect her—that's all."

"She is respectable," he said. "And unattainable. I doubt either one of us could get her if we tried."

Don't smile. Don't fucking smile.

"I'm not sure what's the big deal about Thorn. He's handsome and rich—but so are we."

"I don't get it either."

His eyes drifted back to the blonde over my shoulder. "She's been making eyes at me all night. I'm gonna go for it."

"What about the woman you were with last night?"

"Tanya?" he asked. "She already left for Milan." He grabbed his glass and finished the wine. He threw another hundred-dollar bill on the table. "I've always hated an empty bed. They aren't made for one person." He excused himself and joined her table, taking a seat in the chair beside her. She was with a girlfriend, so maybe he'd end up with both of them at the end of the night.

I paid the rest of the tab and dragged my hand down my face. I'd had a ridiculous outburst with my brother, saying something I should have kept to myself. Titan wasn't ignorant. She knew every man stared at her ass the second she walked away. Did she care? She probably couldn't care less.

So why did I?

———

I GOT MY TEST RESULTS.

I was clean.

I already knew I was clean before I even walked into the doctor's office. I'd been checked six months' prior for my own knowledge. I always wore a condom when I fucked a girl, not just for health reasons but because you never knew who was a nutcase. A lot of women would like to be knocked up by me, to be bound to me with a baby in the mix.

But that wouldn't be an issue with Titan.

I got an extra copy from the doctor, a sealed envelope so she would know I didn't mess with the results. She'd have to be insanely paranoid to have the thought even cross her mind, but this was Tatum Titan.

She needed control in everything.

I texted her after I hit the gym and showered. *I got my results.* Another thing I liked about Titan was the conversation. For a woman, she didn't talk much. She said exactly what she needed to say and left her musings to herself.

It was simpler that way.

She texted me back instantly. *I have mine too.*

I was tired of waiting for her to make up her mind. She went back and forth, comfortable with the arrangement before it terrified her again. We both knew she was going to say yes, so she just needed to shut up and do it. *Then I'm coming by. When I arrive, the only word I better hear out of your mouth is yes.*

Without waiting for a response, I got into the back seat of my car, and my driver took me down the road. If I was willing to meet her end of the bargain, she shouldn't struggle to meet mine. We were both two of the most powerful people in the world. We were compromising—for each other.

When I reached the elevator, I hit the button.

She immediately allowed me entrance, letting the elevator rise to the very top floor where her penthouse was located. Music played in the elevator, and the car slowly came to a stop when I reached the top.

My heart didn't beat fast or slow.

It didn't beat at all.

The doors opened gradually, revealing her standing there with a white envelope in her hand.

I stepped out, extending my envelope just when the doors shut behind me.

We exchanged letters and ripped them open.

Hers checked out even though I'd already known it would.

She must have been satisfied with mine because she shoved it back into the envelope and tossed it on the couch.

My eyes went to hers, silently commanding the answer I craved. "Make me yours and be mine."

Five feet were between us, and she stood with her arms across her chest. Her eyes shifted back and forth as she looked into mine, her gaze unsteady but stern at the same time. She finally lowered her arms to her sides and stepped into me, breaking the distance and replacing it with heated proximity. "Yes."

Finally.

I had the answer I wanted.

Tatum Titan, the most powerful in the world, was officially mine.

And I was also hers.

My hands glided into her hair, and I kissed with shocking passion. I knew I wanted her, was hard in the elevator before the doors even opened, but the desperation that seeped from my flesh still surprised me.

My fingers felt her soft strands of hair, and I cradled her head in my palms. My mouth moved against hers, broke apart, and then moved in again, this time with tongue.

Her hands slid to my wrists where she gripped them tightly, securing them in place with her forceful grip.

I kissed her differently from how I had before, knowing this round would be nothing like all the others. Now I was the only man in her life, the only one she opened her legs for. My name would be the only one on her lips, erupting with a scream when I made her come.

Her soft kisses turned into heated embraces. She devoured me harshly, her small teeth nicking against mine when she turned more aggressive. Her hands moved over my body, gripping my t-shirt and stretching the cotton. She kept pulling on it until she got the shirt over my shoulders and off my head. She moved for my jeans next, unfastening the belt and the button. When she jerked my jeans and boxers down, she sank to her knees along with my clothes.

Then she shoved my dick into her mouth.

Fuck me.

She gripped the base with her slender fingertips

and worked her throat over my length, taking every inch of me like it wasn't a struggle.

And judging from the way others gagged and cried, it was definitely a struggle.

She licked from the base to the tip, treating me like a succulent treat she got at the ice cream shop. Her eyes locked on mine as she made love to my cock, kissing him and lavishing him with the same kisses she'd just given to my mouth.

My hand moved into her hair even though I didn't need to guide her. I just needed something to hold on to, something to keep me balanced. This moment was real—and I was the luckiest asshole on the goddamn planet.

Tatum Titan was sucking my dick.

And she was enjoying it too.

No woman had ever given me head the way she did. She was a pro, a professional courtesan without the experience. Like she was a man who knew exactly what felt good, she sucked my dick just the way I liked. She knew what to do with her hand, her tongue, and her mouth.

She gave my cock a final kiss on the head before she rose to her feet. "In the bedroom. Now." She turned around and strutted away, her pencil skirt making her ass look incredible. It swayed from side to side in the sexiest way.

Instead of being annoyed at the command, I felt a jolt of arousal. This powerful woman wanted to use me, to tell me precisely how to please her. She was so aware of her own sexuality that she wasn't afraid to tell me exactly what she wanted.

Unlike most women. "Yes."

She turned around, her eyes fiery. "Yes, Boss Lady."

I tried not to smile at the name, finding it a perfect fit for this woman.

She placed her hands on her hips, still looking at me with her form of wrath. "That's how you'll address me from now on."

It had a nice ring to it. "Yes, Boss Lady."

Her body relaxed when I obeyed, and she walked into the bedroom that was appointed to her specific tastes. The bed was always made with a dozen decorative pillows. There was a vase of fresh flowers on the nightstand. Throughout her house and the bathrooms, there were always fresh flowers sprinkled everywhere.

It was obviously one of her touches.

She unzipped her skirt and peeled off her clothes,

getting everything off until she was naked just the way I was.

I wouldn't mind any position tonight. However we did it, it would feel incredible. My pulsing cock was desperate to be inside her bareback. That tight and wet pussy would be nothing but erotic flesh. I could dump all of my come inside her, filling her up until it overflowed.

Fuck, I wasn't gonna last long at this rate.

She moved on the bed, her back to the comforter.

I immediately crawled on top of her, not wanting to waste a second longer than I had to. I was glad we were face-to-face because I wanted to watch her come to the feeling of my bare dick.

Her legs locked around my waist, and her arms moved around my neck. "Not yet."

I growled against her mouth.

She kissed me the way she did in the living room, rough and hard. Her fingers massaged my muscles, her nails teasing me with their sharpness. When she pulled me into her body, she ground her soaked pussy against my length.

Hot damn.

Her ankles locked together, and she continued to move, rolling her hips in the sexiest way. She turned her lips away from my mouth and pressed them to my

VICTORIA QUINN

ear, still working her clit against my dick. "When I say, I want you to fuck me hard, Hunt. I want it to be deep and fast…deeper and harder than you've ever fucked anyone else."

I kissed her neck, my tongue running across her pulse. "Yes, Boss Lady." My hand dug into her hair, and I got a tight grip on her, keeping her perfectly positioned underneath me. I was going to rock her world so hard that she would lose her voice from screaming. She was going to be so sore that she couldn't walk the next day.

The kissing and touching continued, and she made me wait.

Kept making me wait.

My cock was so hard, already smothered in her lubrication. Slick sounds erupted between our body parts, our arousals as loud as a drum. I couldn't stop imagining how she would feel, how that slick pussy would feel once I was buried inside her. She was amazing through a condom. I couldn't fathom how she would feel with nothing between us.

Nothing.

"Woman, let me fuck you." I spoke into her mouth, my body shaking because I was so hard up. I could barely breathe, my body was so weak. I was melting right on top of her, my mind sinking into a pool of pure sex.

She tucked my bottom lip into her mouth. "You want to fuck me, Hunt?"

I ground my cock against her folds. "More than anything."

"You want to give me your come?"

All I could do was moan. Coherent words weren't possible right now.

"Tell me you want to come inside me."

I breathed through my teeth, my spine tightening. "I want to come inside you…until you can't hold any more."

She dragged her nails down my back before she widened her legs, opening herself up to me. "Then give it to me."

Halle-fucking-lujah.

I grabbed my base and pointed my head into her entrance, feeling the moisture pooling for me. I pushed through it, feeling her tight flesh surround me. My eyes were glued to hers, watching her eyes widen and her cheeks flush at my entrance. I inched farther, feeling more of her slickness, more of her tightness.

Fuck. Fuck. Fuck.

I slid all the way inside, sheathing myself until only my balls were outside her body. I'd been this deep inside her before, but it felt like a completely different experience now.

This pussy was mine.

Her breathing hitched, and she gripped my biceps as she held on to me. Her flushed chest rose and fell with her deep breathing, and her small tongue could be seen through her slightly parted teeth.

I was completely buried inside her—and I never wanted to leave. "Titan…"

She slapped me across the face, a gentle tap. "Boss Lady."

I loved the tingling sensation that ensued when her small palm smacked against my skin. I loved the initial contact, the burn, and the heat. I'd never been slapped by a woman, and now I realized it was a huge turn-on. Or maybe it was just a turn-on because Titan could pull it off. "Boss Lady…"

"Now, fuck me." She grabbed my hips and pulled me inside her.

I hooked my arms behind her knees and thrust into her, hard every single time.

She moaned right away, releasing feminine cries every time my cock pushed deep within her. "Deeper…"

I folded her body until she was pinned to the bed. I rammed her at the deepest angle I could, forcing my nine inches to go in as deep as possible. It baffled me how such a petite woman could handle it, but she obviously knew how she liked to take cock.

"Yes…" Her nails dug into my chest, and she lolled her head back.

I worked up a sweat thrusting into her, feeling the slickness between our two bodies. My cock could feel every intimate detail of her channel, sensations I hadn't been exposed to with a rubber around my length. But now I could feel everything, touch everything. Pussy was even better than I thought it was.

It was fucking crack.

I moaned under my breath, my body falling into the ecstasy just as my mind was. Every thrust was so good. She was getting wetter and tighter. My cock was covered in her lubrication, piling up at the base of my cock and underneath the ridge at the head of my cock.

"Faster…" She yanked on my waist, directing me inside her.

All the muscles in my body worked together to give her what she wanted, to fuck her at a speed that was bound to break her bed. I was giving it to her deep and fast, and soon was I panting from the exertion.

I'd never fucked this hard in my life.

"God…yes." She closed her eyes as her beautiful mouth opened. Her nipples were hard and her tits were firm. "You're gonna make me come, Hunt."

Damn right, I am.

"But you aren't going to come until I say so."

Fuck, why did she have to tease me? I fucking hated it, but I loved it. The wait was always torture, but the explosion was always powerful.

She dug her nails into me and breathed deeper, harder.

She tightened around my length. I was already used to the sensation, but now it was strong than before. Her pussy had the strength of a metal crusher. She gripped me tighter than my own hand did when I jerked off.

Then she let out a scream that would make me come if I allowed myself to.

"Hunt…Hunt…yes."

I wanted to come so damn bad. Listening to a woman like Titan call out my name in bed was the sexiest thing I'd ever heard.

I kept going, grinding my body against her clit to make the climax last longer. Sweat was heavy across my skin, making her hands slip when she tried to grip me tightly. My mind and my cock kept thinking about releasing inside her. I wanted to watch that white come drip between her ass cheeks and to the bed beneath her.

I wanted to admire my handiwork.

But she didn't let me.

She made me keep going, made me keep fucking her and making her come. Over and over again, I brought her to heaven and gave her a taste of the clouds. Over and over, I had to watch her enjoy me without being able to join her.

I couldn't hold on much longer. I couldn't do it.

I was strong—but I wasn't invincible.

When she'd had her third orgasm, she cupped my face and kissed me. "You earned it, Hunt. Give it to me.

Fuck yeah.

I pounded her hard again, only lasting five seconds before I hit my threshold. I shoved my entire length inside her, hitting her cervix, and I came.

I came so hard.

And I came so much.

"Fuck…" I pressed my forehead to hers as I finished, having this beautiful woman wide open to take me. The orgasm seemed to go on forever, stretching on and on. I wasn't sure how much I gave her, but I knew it was mounds worth. "Fuck."

She hooked her ankles together around my waist and kept me buried inside her. "So heavy…so warm."

I thrust gently as I started to soften, feeling my come and hers mix together.

She kissed the corner of my mouth then ran her hands through my hair, her fingers getting coated in my sweat. "I want more." She kissed the corner of my mouth again, kissing me softly after being so aggressive with me.

"I'll give you more."

———

AN HOUR LATER, we lay in her bed together, naked and spent.

My view on the world was completely different now. I'd had a lot of great sex in my life, been with a lot of gorgeous women, but fuck, I didn't know anything until now. Now I'd been with a real woman, been with someone who wasn't afraid to be sexy and adventurous.

And her pussy…Jesus Christ.

She crawled on top of me and sprinkled kisses on my chest. "I had fun tonight."

"I did too." My hand trailed up her smooth back, cupping the back of her neck.

"You're quite the lover." She kissed the skin over my heart before she got out of bed and pulled a t-shirt over her head.

"Nothing compared to you."

She smiled before she grabbed a fresh pair of panties from her drawer. "I don't know about that…" She glanced at the clock before she turned back to me. "You should get going. It's getting late."

I'd never slept over before, and I suspected she didn't want me to. "How about I stay here with you?"

Her gaze turned hard. "Because I don't want you to."

Wow. Talk about giving it to me straight. I kicked the sheets aside then started to get dressed. "Ever?"

"Ever." She left the bedroom and walked to the front of her penthouse.

After I pulled on my shirt, I followed her. "Any reason why?"

She ignored the question altogether and stopped at the elevator. "Good night."

I didn't like to cuddle with women. I'd always been the kind of guy who needed the whole bed to myself. Whenever a woman stayed, she hogged the sheets and then spent the following day lounging around my house. And I couldn't be an asshole and ask her to leave.

Now the tables had been turned.

She didn't want me to linger. She just wanted me to fuck and leave.

Fine by me. "Good night." I leaned down and kissed her on the lips.

She wrapped her arms around me and kissed me harder, giving me some of her tongue.

For having just asked me to leave, it didn't seem like she wanted me to go anywhere.

She finally ended the kiss and stepped back. "Bye, Hunt."

The elevator doors opened, inviting me inside.

I stared at her for several heartbeats, confounded by this woman. She was the most passionate lover I'd ever had, but she could turn off that lust instantly. She could ask me to leave without feeling the least bit guilty about it.

I stepped inside then turned around. I looked at her deep brown hair, her green eyes, and her pretty face. She was a ruthless dictator, but she had a profoundly womanly touch. She was so soft, so easy on the eyes. She was so beautiful it hurt to look at her sometimes. But those amazing features and soft skin didn't show what was really underneath. "Bye, Boss Lady."

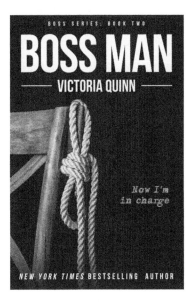

I've never made a compromise before.

But I made an exception for Diesel Hunt.

Because he was all man. Because he was everything I needed. Because he would make it worth my while.

Now I'm calling the shots. I'm the one in control. No matter how much I hurt him, he asks for more.

All I can think about is when my turns arrives.

When I'm the one on my knees, wrists bound.

Completely powerless to this man.

Diesel Hunt...the most powerful man in the world.

Hartwick Publishing

As insatiable romance readers, we love great stories. But we want original romance novels that have something special - something that we'll remember even after turning the last page. That's how Hartwick Publishing came into being. We promise to bring you beautiful stories that are unlike any other on the market - and that already have millions of fans.

With its New York Times best-selling authors, Hartwick Publishing is unparalleled. Our focus is not on the authors, but on you as a reader!

Join Hartwick Publishing by signing up for our newsletter! As a thank you for joining our family, you will receive the first volume of the Obsidian Series (Black Obsidian) for free directly into your email inbox!

http://eepurl.com/cpt7mv

Printed in Great Britain
by Amazon